Trials

C000185878

Amanda Vi

Cover design by rebecacovers©

Contents

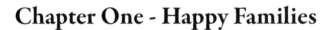

Chapter One - Happy Families

"*Happy birthday to you!*" rang out the voices in unison. Looking around at the faces present, I was so thankful for the many years of happiness that we had been blessed with. I couldn't believe that my twins were now five! Five years old, and they were adorable.

Mason, with his vibrant auburn hair and cheeky grin, made us all laugh and smile every day, and Madison - well, as predicted, she turned out to be a little diva. She was the mirror image of Stephen, and every time I looked at her, I could see her daddy staring up at me. Madison always got her own way, but I don't think the fact that she was 'daddy's little girl' helped with the whole scenario.

Then there was Henry, our cute little three year old, who had just emerged from the 'terrible twos'. In looks, he was a mix of the twins, but bless him, he was always pushed to the side-lines by them. They loved each other to pieces but if there was a toy fight going on, then Madison and Mason would join forces to get it back. Natalie was a saint a put up with it, and I always thought it took a special kind of person to want to work, and live, as a nanny with children. They all loved her, and it was a pleasure to witness the bond between them.

So today was the day of Madison and Mason's fifth birthday, and all the family were around at the house. The garden was lined with tables and balloons, as the twins had invited all their friends from school over for a huge party. Entertainers were twisting long balloons into balloon animals, while there was face painting, nail painting, makeup, and all manner of things going on to dress up the little ones who were present.

Some of the other parents had stuck around to help monitor their child, but some of them had just dropped off their bundles of joy for us to keep an eye out for. I didn't blame them - even though we were lucky enough to have a nanny, I still wouldn't have minded five minutes peace here or there from the chaos of the party.

Another child that was present, was Tasha's little boy, Reece. Reece was a cheeky little chappy, and just a few months older than Henry, they got on really well. I was glad that Henry had a little playmate. He needed that when he was pushed out onto the side-lines by Madison and Mason, who they were stuck together like glue.

David was back on the scene, and although him and Tasha were not officially a couple, me and Stephen had our suspicions that they were 'hooking up' every now and then. But they were both consenting adults, so there's nothing much we could do about it. David seemed to have cleaned up his act, and while that was a relief and we could forgive what he had put us through, we could never forget. The stint in rehab had served him well, and he seemed to be calmer since he'd been weaned off the white stuff.

"Happy anniversary, beautiful." Stephen smiled, as he wrapped an arm around my waist, and gave me a little kiss on the cheek as we watched the children eat their party food.

"Happy anniversary, handsome." I smiled back, leaning into his presence and realizing that I'd almost completely forgotten it was our day too. The prediction of our anniversaries being filled with balloons and birthday cake, had certainly come true.

'I've gotten you a little surprise," he whispered into my ear.

I turned to look at him. "Oh, really? I'll be honest, organizing this party, I've forgotten to get you anything!" I laughed.

"Don't worry about it. There'll be plenty more to come." He winked, before turning back to the garden full of hyped-up children.

"I'll have to get you an even bigger gift next year." I winked back.

"No need. You know I have all I need with you. I love you." He grinned.

"I love you, too."

Just as we stood and practically ignored our surroundings, we were interrupted by a voice:

"Eleanor, sweetheart, I'll have to get going soon. I've got to run over the accounts for the new order." Clarisse smiled.

"Aw, that's no worries. It can wait, though, if you want to stay longer, Mom?" I offered.

"I would leave it, but with the Rose Design expansion, I know we are on a time limit with this."

"Yeah, agreed. I could really do with working now, but until Henry, Madison, and Mason have gone to bed, I really don't think I'll have chance." I chuckled, watching Natalie pull a burst balloon from Henry's little hand.

"That's what I'm here for. You enjoy the party. It's been lovely. Those beautiful grandchildren of mine are a delight," Clarisse beamed towards them.

"Thanks so much, Mom... and for helping organize this. I couldn't have done it without you." I smiled, bringing her into a warm hug.

"My pleasure. I want to be a part of everything. I missed way too much," she replied sadly.

"Hey, you're here now, and that's the main thing," I reassured. "Thanks for their gifts as well. Mason absolutely loves the truck you got him."

"I think he's going to be into construction when he's older... not sure if there'll be any room for design." She chuckled.

"A master in construction would be really helpful right now, with the expansion." I smiled.

"Yes, very true. Anyway, I'll say goodbye to the children and head off."

"That's fine. Thanks so much for coming. If you need me for anything, though, just call and I'll check over any details. Give some of the work over to the accounts team if it's too much."

"It's fine. I like knowing that everything is as it should be. I can't get out of the habit of a lifetime." She chuckled.

"Me neither. I seem to be in full throttle of chasing my father's legacy." I grinned.

"He would be so proud. Anyway, I better go. I'll see you soon."

Clarisse brought me into a hug, before making her way over to the children to say goodbye. She was a model mom and grandmother, and I wasn't sure what I would have done without her over the past few years. Clarisse was amazing, and it was the best thing that had ever happened to me, when I'd found out that she was my birth mom.

Checking my watch, I realized that it was 5pm. The party would be over soon, and a large part of me sighed with relief at that notion. Whoever invented children's parties was probably drunk, because apart from when it was over, it wasn't much fun for the adults. I'd spent the day making sure that all the children were sharing, there were no tears, and that I wouldn't be handing unhappy children back to their parents at the end of it.

As I stood there, eyeing the masses of children who had now finished eating and were dancing around to the music booming over the speakers, threatening to throw up the remnants of their dinner, Tasha and Jeanie wandered over to me, with Tasha carrying Reece in her arms.

"Aw, is the little guy worn out?" I asked, eyeing the drooping child on Tasha's shoulder.

"Yeah... he missed his nap this afternoon, so he's threatening to sleep now." She sighed.

"We'll be up all night if you let him sleep now, Tash. Just wiggle him about a bit to keep him awake," Jeanie prompted.

"It has been that kind of day. I think we'll all sleep tonight." I chuckled, watching Stephen throw a few shapes with his daughter on the dancefloor.

Jeanie turned to look at what I was watching. "Hmm, although some of us have more energy than sense." She laughed.

"It's all those protein shakes he's drinking at the moment. Ever since becoming a physiotherapist he's taken fitness to the extreme!" I laughed, shaking my head at the sight of him singing along to "Barbie Girl" by Aqua with Madison.

Jeanie laughed. "I might try one of those if it makes me more energetic."

"Penny's going around the bend with it. She keeps complaining about having to make them instead of her infamous smoothies. One day she'll throttle him with a blender." I sniggered.

"Where is Penny? And Roger?" Tasha wondered, trying to haul Reece up who seemed to be turning into a lead weight.

"Roger is away with Ross this weekend. I gave Penny the day off while this party was going on. She's gone to visit her daughters. Otherwise I knew that she would've wanted to cater this whole party, so I was freeing her of losing her sanity in a garden full of five year old's." I grinned.

Stephen, puffed out and looking like a beetroot, made his way over to where we were standing.

"Geez, those kids could give anyone a run for their money!" He laughed, and then turned to Tasha. "He looks tired, Tash. Get yourselves home and let him have half an hour."

"I might actually let him have a little sleep." Tasha grinned. "I think David wants to have him tonight."

"Are you still sure about letting David have joint custody?" Stephen frowned, his jaw slightly clenching at the thought.

"Yeah, he's fine now that he's sorted himself out," Tasha pouted.

Looking at Reece, he was David's double, and there was no denying that he was the father of Tasha's baby. I sometimes looked at our little nephew and prayed that he would turn out nothing like his father. David had been on his very best behavior for the past three years, so even though we were all waiting for a slip-up of some sort, we knew we had to let it go.

"Aw, well it'll be nice for him to spend some time with his daddy." I smiled softly, noting the look of wonder in Stephen's eyes, but knowing that it was really about time we moved on.

"Yeah, he's great with Reece!" Tasha beamed, seemingly pleased that I was on board with things.

"Hmm, I still keep a very close eye on him." Jeanie frowned.

"So do I," Stephen agreed.

Just as Tasha was about to protest to the 'David hating club' that was occurring, the doorbell interrupted our conversation. I was relieved to be saved by the bell, as I vacated the tense atmosphere that was being created, and made my way to the front door. It was some of the parent's starting to arrive to collect their little ones, so I showed them through while they asked the mandatory questions to their child, of whether they'd had a nice time and been good, while I gave out goody bags to each of them.

One by one, the children started to stream out of the front door, and left Madison, Mason, and Henry to their own devices, skipping around the remnants of party poppers and streamers that were strewn on the grass - generally thinking that the mess was wonderful. While they acted like they didn't have a care in the world, Tasha left to take Reece home, and Jeanie stayed behind with me and Stephen to clean up. The catering staff and party people cleared away their belongings, and I made sure that all finances were settled and thanked them for their services.

All-in-all, the children had had a great time, and even though I could've bellyached about my aching feet, it was well worth the effort. Natalie said that she would take the twins and Henry upstairs to bathe them and settle them down before their bedtime, so I gave them all a kiss and a cuddle before she took them up. Seeing the look of tiredness, yet sheer happiness on the faces of

my babies was priceless, and something that I could never have taken for grant-
ed.

"I'll be going now, kids!" Jeanie announced, as she hauled her tenth bag of
garbage into the trash.

"Thanks so much for your help." I smiled, wandering over from where I was
clearing up to give her a hug.

"You're welcome. You did a great job today, Eleanor." She smiled back.

"The kids are thrilled with their gifts, and thank you for coming today,"
Stephen remarked, making his way over.

"I've had a great day," Jeanie beamed. "Now, I better go... if David is collecting Reece tonight, I want to make sure I give him the third degree before he
leaves." She winked, collecting her purse and heading toward the front door.

Stephen skipped ahead and opened the door for her. "Love you, Mom." He
smiled, giving her a kiss on the cheek.

"Love you too, son," she replied, then turned her attention to me. "Love
you, Eleanor. Enjoy your evening, you two! I'll see you in work on Monday!"
she called back, as she headed out of the door and to her car.

"Bye, Jeanie!" I shouted, as we both stood and waved to her as she drove
out of the driveway.

When Jeanie had disappeared from view, Stephen closed the door and leant
back on it.

"What a day!" He sighed, resting his eyes on me. "You ready for your surprise?"

My eyes lit up. "Yes! Show me!" I chuckled, as he grabbed my hand and led
me through the hallway and into the living area.

Sitting down on the sofa, I watched as he walked over to the side-cabinet
in the room and removed a small box from the draw, closing it behind him and
then grinning at me.

"Hope you like it." He smiled, as he came and sat down next to me and
handed me the box.

Grinning excitedly at him, I took the box and wondered what it could be.
We were already married, so it's not like it was going to be an engagement ring
or anything like that - I was intrigued. I lifted the lid of the small velvet box, to
reveal a stunning, platinum eternity ring, with a band of diamonds, and right
in the centre was a little pearl peeping through.

"Oh, Stephen! That's beautiful!" I gasped, as I removed it from the box, placing it on my finger above my wedding ring.

"I had it specially made. Something to remind you that my love for you is eternal."

I could've melted on the spot. He was the sweetest man on the planet, and in all the years we had been together, I hadn't doubted that for a second, but he still never ceased to amaze me.

"I absolutely love it," I beamed, turning to him and softly kissing his lips.

He pulled away and smiled playfully. "I got you something else as well."

Even more intrigued than before, I watched him rise from the sofa again, and wander back over to the cabinet; this time retrieving a larger, slenderer box from inside a different draw.

"Are you just hiding stuff around the house?" I chuckled, as he brought the next box over to me.

As I unwrapped it, he turned to me. "This one, I will admit, is more for me." He grinned.

Opening up the box, inside was a lacy black garment - one that didn't really leave much to the imagination.

"Ah, I see what you mean." I chuckled. "Looks like I didn't really have to buy anything for you."

Stephen's eyes lit up. "No, that is enough present for me. I knew you hadn't remembered, but it's really no problem. You've been so busy lately, so I thought it would be nice if we had some quality time together. I feel like I've hardly seen you."

"Yeah, I know what you mean. Sorry about that," I replied sadly.

"Hey, it's not your fault. You're doing so well with the business." He smiled, taking hold of my hand in his.

I did feel guilty about how much I had been working. I'd always strived to have a steady work-life balance, yet recently, with the expansion of Rose Designs, I hadn't had a minute to think. I had neglected Stephen, and even though he had been busy with his own job and pursuing his own dreams, I didn't want him to feel like he was being ignored.

"Shall I go and try this on?" I grinned, holding it up from the box.

"I'm not going to say no to that." He chuckled.

"Come on..." I laughed, as I dropped the box and took Stephen's hand in mine.

Like the love-struck couple we used to be, and garment in hand, we raced upstairs together laughing, but becoming a little quieter passing Natalie's room. Locking the bedroom door behind us, I went to slip into something a little more uncomfortable, as Stephen waited for me on the bed. As I changed in the ensuite, I thought back to how things used to be. It was amazing how the years could change the intensity of a relationship. Years ago, I wouldn't have even made it into the ensuite before we were all over each other. I supposed that now things had settled down, and it was unrealistic to think that everything would always stay that way.

As I emerged from the bathroom, Stephen looked over at me; the sheer glee of me wearing something that could barely cover my ass, filling him with delight. It did make me chuckle inside about how self-conscious I still was. I wish I had been more body-confident before I'd had three children, but hindsight was a wonderful thing - especially when you didn't have a time machine.

Stephen didn't seem to mind, though, as he made love to me. It did feel wonderful to be back in my loving husbands arms. The arms that for all those years had made me feel protected and loved. As we lay back afterwards, I looked at my left hand which was now donning the eternity ring, and that was one thing I would always be certain of - my love for this utterly beautiful man.

Chapter Two - Moral Support

A blissful weekend ensued. Me and Stephen spent some much-needed time together on Saturday before Natalie had the day off on Sunday and we looked after the children. I loved watching them play - even though Henry spent most of his time trying to break through the bond that Madison and Mason had - but we tried to make sure that they were playing fairly.

When the Sunday evening approached, we put the children to bed and sat together in the living room, flicking on the television, and wondering whether I could pause time and not have to work tomorrow. Things were full on with the expansion, and I was definitely going to make sure that we booked a vacation when things had settled down. As we sat back and relished in the peace and quiet, my cell went off with a buzz in my pocket.

"That's probably my mom with something work related." I sighed, as I pulled the cell out of my pocket to take a look.

"Clarisse works too hard," Stephen replied, as he channel-hopped through various shows.

Smirking at the truth of his statement, I glanced at him looking like he never had a care in the world, while most of the time I had something going on in my head. It would've been nice to have been able to switch off like he did.

Unlocking my cell, I noticed that it wasn't Clarisse texting me, it was Tasha, with quite an unusual request. The message read:

Hi Eleanor, just a quick one. Was wondering, David has received a message from his sister. She wants to see him - apparently it's been years. He didn't want to ask you himself because he felt a bit embarrassed, but he wondered whether we would go with him? You know, moral support. I would've text Stevie, but I know he'll say no. Let me know xx

Squinting at the screen, I tried to process what had just been asked of me. David was seeing his sister that he hadn't seen in years, yet he wanted us to go and support him? Why? Surely for something like that you would've just gone by yourself. Before I could relay any information to Stephen - who would definitely say no - I text Tasha back.

Hey Tash, why does he want us to go with him? Can't you go with Reece? Xx

Moments later, she text back:

I know it's strange, but she is having a yacht party and wanted us to go. She wanted to know what he's been up to all these years. He's mentioned names to her, and I think he's a little bit embarrassed about how things have turned out. So considering we are all pretty much settled now, he'd like us all to be there. I think to prove a point that he's not completely messed everything up. You are Reece's aunt and uncle, so I'd really like you to be there for me too. I don't know her xx

I sighed as I replied:

Fine. I'll speak to Stephen. I don't know what he'll say. When is this yacht party? Xx

I waited for the buzz of a reply:

It's on Tuesday at 7:30pm! I know it's short notice, but I only just found out. She's flying in from New York tomorrow xx

I replied:

I didn't realize David's family lived in New York? Xx

Tasha replied:

Apparently they moved there years ago. David's parents still don't want to see him, but his sister is keen to get in touch. As much as he won't admit it, I think he does miss his family. Plus he has spoken about everyone, so I think his sister just wants to meet us xx

I thought about it for a moment. The more 'normal' David that we knew now probably did harbor those kinds of feelings, and I could see where he was coming from. Also, if his sister had been told tales about us and what had gone on, I'd probably want to meet us too.

Fine, Tash. I'll speak to Stephen and let you know. Xx

She text me back and thanked me, as I sat awkwardly next to Stephen, who was now watching a movie that I wasn't paying a blind bit of attention to. How was I going to ask him this?

"Oh yeah, would you come and meet my ex-sister-in-law? None of us know her, but it could be fun." Yeah, that wasn't going to wash.

"Everything all right, Eleanor?" Stephen asked, breaking up my mind-haze, and obviously picking up on the fact that I had probably tensed up sat next to him.

"Er, yeah," I replied, trying to look normal. "That was Tasha," I informed him, referring to the texts.

"Tasha? What did she want?" Stephen eyed, looking like he was wondering if he had to go and pound down on someone for hurting his sister.

"Right," I composed myself and turned to him. "Now hear me out..."

"What is it?" Stephen abruptly asked, obviously not giving me much chance of easing him into the idea of this.

"She text me about David..."

"What has that idiot done now? I swear to God, Eleanor..." Stephen's face was doing that red-mist thing again, so I knew I had to spit it out.

"He hasn't done anything!" I quickly cut in, putting the man out of his misery. "It's just that his sister wants to see him... there's this yacht party on Tuesday. He wants us to go with him."

Stephen started laughing, as I looked on at him like he had obviously lost the plot.

"Why are you laughing?" I eyed curiously.

"Why in the world does he want us to go with him? He's obviously still living on planet loopy! You sure he's clean?" he mused to himself.

"Stephen, come on. We have to give him half a chance now. We've had no problems from him since he went into rehab."

"I still don't trust him," Stephen snapped.

"I know, but they have Reece now, and we have to at least try for our nephew's sake. You don't want Reece around any friction over his dad when he's older, do you?" I asked, trying to appeal to his softer side.

Stephen eased, still pulling a face about it. "No, I suppose not. So why does Psycho-Sommers, er, I mean, David, want us to go?" He frowned.

"Here... instead of me explaining, read the texts from Tasha."

Handing my cell phone over to Stephen, I watched on as he read over them. When he had finished, he handed my cell back over to me.

"Hmm... I don't know. Why would he need us there for that? It doesn't make sense." He frowned.

"I agree. But it's only for some support... he hasn't got anyone else. Plus, I think Tasha wants us there as well, more for her." I laughed. "It'll only be for a couple of hours, so why not? At least we'll be building bridges. It may help David more, having his family around."

Stephen sighed. "I'm not really in the mood for helping him out, but I'll go for Tasha. If David is anything to go by, then I'm not having both her and Reece surrounded by two psychos."

"That's the spirit!" I sarcastically laughed. "One big happy family!"

"Hmm... one big mess," he sulked, as he turned his attention back to the television.

Texting Tasha back, I told her that we would be there. It might've been nice to have a little rendezvous on a yacht with Stephen, as it had been years since I'd been to a yacht party, and I used to love them. Although I doubted that this one would consist of bikini dancing and drinking shots from the half-naked waiters - but whatever, I was game.

For the rest of the night we sat in relative silence. I could tell that Stephen was mulling over the prospect of attending the impromptu party, but he wanted to keep Tasha safe, and that was his excuse for going.

Also, I think he was a bit peeved at me for saying that we would go. I did think it was odd that David wanted us there and his sister wanted to meet us, but I could kind of see why he wanted some support. I'm not sure how David had left things with his family, or what sort of relationship he had with his sister, but I liked to think that if I needed some moral support in such a situation, people around me would help me out. To be fair, I think we both were mainly going for Tasha and Reece's benefit, but there was no point in putting any more thought into it - we were going, and that was that.

THE NEXT DAY I WAS up bright and early to get to work on time. Everything was so hectic, and I was glad to leave the 'David and his sister' dilemma behind. Stephen had gone into his 'man cave', and I was glad to escape the grunts and half-answers that I was receiving in reply to almost everything.

Entering Rose Designs, Clarisse was sitting in her usual spot in reception, as I breezily wandered through.

"Morning, Mom!" I called out to her, and it still to this day seemed a little strange at calling Clarisse, Mom, but I had taken to the idea of it a lot more easily since I had found out that my fake-mom was a nutcase.

"Morning, Eleanor!" she called back, her head buried in her laptop. "Oh, that reminds me!" she shouted, darting up from her station and making her way over to me.

"What is it?" I eyed warily as she practically sprinted toward me.

"Oh, nothing to worry about." She chuckled. "I have a message for you."

Clarisse handed me a printout of an email she'd received.

I looked over it in my hand. "It's from our new contact, Brandon Corporation. What do they want?" I asked, before I got to reading the end of it.

"Well, you know they want all the new designs from us?" I nodded at Clarisse. "On Wednesday, there is a meeting at a local restaurant. They are keen to meet you face-to-face and discuss what's required."

"Face-to-face? I generally send out a designer for that. Things are pretty busy right now," I grumbled.

"I know, but you know how much business they are bringing our way. The CEO of that company has requested the meeting. I think it's important that you go."

More invitations? Seriously? I was like a busy bee most days, and I could barely keep up with my schedule as it was.

"Fine. What time and at what restaurant?"

"It says at the bottom there. It's 7pm at Florida Bell. I'll send an email back and say that's okay. Do you want me to go with you?" she offered.

"No, it's fine. I'll go and meet this CEO by myself. I can finish up here and eat there before I go home," I stated, not really relishing the thought of having to attend the meal.

Usually one of my design team would meet potential clients and I would be left alone, but considering that Brandon Corporation would potentially be bringing millions to our door, for once I could overlook the lack of enthusiasm that was filling me.

"Anyway, how are the construction workers getting on?" I smiled, clicking back to what was happening in the present moment.

"Great. Come on, I'll show you what they did this morning. They are working wonders on the extension of the building." Clarisse smiled, as she took my arm and we ventured along to where the building contractors were busy at work.

It would only be a few weeks until the extension was ready, and I couldn't wait to see it. Me and Clarisse had also bought another building further into the heart of California, and that was also under construction, ready to be opened up for more contracts to come flooding in. It would also open up a wealth of jobs, and a lot more business for us.

Since Bryant's demise, and his wife Caroline's help, we had been snowed under with new clientele, and everything was going so well. It was nice to be safe in the knowledge that business was booming, because as soon as the expansion was done, I would be able to take some time out and focus more on home life.

I couldn't wait to spend a lot more of my time with Stephen and the children, and let somebody else take the reins on this place. I'd told Clarisse that as soon as I took a backseat, she would be expected to do so as well. She always worked so hard, and instead, she could spend more time with myself and the children, and have more of a life instead of working all the time. I wasn't sure whether that idea sat well with her, but I knew that she needed a break, and should reap the rewards of all her hard work.

After checking out the building work that had been done, I ventured through to the office that I had set up for Jeanie. Jeanie was fantastic with design work, and was another lady who liked to work more than to be told to have a day off. I'd placed her in charge of the bespoke rose designs that went out on all sorts of household furnishings. She had such an eye for it, and she knew what I liked. Our bespoke range was flying out of the doors, and I thanked my lucky stars that I had Jeanie on board - she was another mom who was a complete gem.

Jeanie was happy, checking over designs for some canvas prints that were due to be made up, and all was ticking along nicely. I loved the fact that it was a real family business. Tasha had done a bit more modeling for some website photo's that I'd asked for, but she seemed to like to stay at home more with Reece - getting up to goodness-knows-what with David. David was paying child support, and now that he was working back in design for some other company, he was earning the wage to enable Tasha to be a stay-at-home-mom.

The working day flew by quickly, as I made my way through the reams of emails, phone calls, and generally sorting out each department that'd had some downtime over the weekend. It never ceased to amaze me, that even though we generally had weekends off, the build up from those two days, first thing on a Monday, was catastrophic.

At the end of another tiring day, I dragged myself back home. My feet were aching, and my back was hurting, yet I still had little to no desire of booking myself in for a massage. When I got back to the house, I parked my car in front of the garages, and went inside to see where everyone was. As I placed my purse at the side of front door in the hallway, I could hear distant laughter coming from the kitchen, so I went to locate where the life was in the house.

"Miss. Eleanor! How was your day, child?" Penny beamed, finishing dishing up food for us to tuck into.

"Tiring, Penny." I sighed, sitting myself next to Stephen on a bar stool at the kitchen island.

"You work so hard!" Penny exclaimed, placing pots and pans into the sink.

"Eleanor, far be it for me to interfere, but why don't you just let someone at your workplace take over?" Stephen commented, chewing on a stick of celery.

"Because I can't right now with this expansion. Plus, on Wednesday, the CEO of a new company we've managed to get a contract with wants to meet with me personally, so there's no chance of taking a back seat at the moment," I pouted.

"Don't you usually send one of your design team out to do that?" Stephen queried, as Penny handed us a plate of food each over the island.

"Yeah, but he wants to see me in person. This is a really high-spec company, and even though we are doing well, what they want, they get." I chuckled, digging into my food.

Stephen shrugged and followed suit, as we sat with Penny and chatted about our days. Stephen was telling us about the clients he'd had today, and whilst he worked for a physiotherapy company and didn't own one - even though I'd offered - I did envy him. He had no extra responsibilities as soon as he clocked off from work, and I did wonder what that freedom was like. I was doing this to leave something behind for our children, though, and that was the goal that I'd always had in mind when I felt like sleeping for a week.

THE TUESDAY DAWNED, and it was an average day of running around like a total nut, but there was one difference tonight which was the yacht party - and meeting David's sister. I did chuckle to myself when I thought about how when we were married, I never once met any of his relatives - apart from Bryant, unfortunately - but now that we were divorced, and he had a child with my sister-in-law, I would get to meet one of them. What a weird scenario it actually was.

When it was close to the time of departure, I got dressed and had Roger do my hair and makeup. Even though I didn't know the woman we were meeting tonight, it was always good to make a decent first impression. I slipped on a nice, red cocktail gown and heels to match, because I knew how fancy these yacht parties were. I wondered to myself what his sister actually did for a living, because in order to have afforded that, she must have been bringing in a good salary. I suppose, even for his flaws, David had never shirked on the work front - even if in his spare time he did like to fleece people of their businesses behind their backs.

Taking one last look in the mirror, I ventured down the stairs. It actually felt nice to be dressed up, as I hadn't had chance to do this a lot lately. Stephen, as usual, was waiting at the bottom of the staircase for me, wearing a lovely crisp shirt and trousers, and he still was so handsome.

"Wow, you look beautiful, Eleanor." He grinned from ear-to-ear.

"Thank you, handsome. You look very nice." I smirked, thinking about how much I could actually rip the shirt off him.

He smirked back at me, and held out his arm for me to link. "Let's go and face the psycho family." He chuckled.

"Oh, that makes me feel so much better about tonight!" I laughed.

Exiting the house, Stephen said that he would drive tonight, as he wanted to keep a clear head in case of any unwanted scenarios. I agreed with him on that one, and it was good that he was keeping his guard up, although I needed a drink just to be there, so I was glad not to be driving.

Stephen opened the door of his car for me, and I sat in the passenger side and wondered if I could go back into the house, get changed and go to bed instead. I wasn't really looking forward to a party tonight because I was always exhausted after work, but it was one of those things that just had to be done, for Tasha, and then that would be it for, hopefully, forever.

We drove along until we reached the harbor which the yacht was supposedly docked in. Apart from looking for Tasha and David, I had no idea what yacht I was looking for. There were several, and I didn't feel like gate-crashing somebody else's night by accident.

The marina was beautiful at this time, and was so picturesque. With the sunset shimmering on the water's surface, I did wonder whether I should invest in a yacht, as it would be great to escape to somewhere like this when I had more spare time.

Stephen parked the car and got out, coming around to the passenger side and helping me out of the vehicle. As he locked the car behind us, we walked along the harbor, with me trying not to get my heels caught in between the slats of the wooden planks.

"Wow, what a place," Stephen remarked, looking around him in awe.

Still to this day, I completely forgot that a lot of this lifestyle was new to him. I'd grown up with all this around me, and never batted an eyelid. But we'd never actually done anything like this together, so it was a brand new experience for him.

"Ah, there's Tasha and David!" I pointed toward a yacht at the end of the harbor - a beautiful, white haven resting on the water ahead.

"Hey, you came!" Tasha shouted toward us, sounding relieved that we had shown up.

"Yes, we said we would." I smiled toward her.

David strode along to us behind her. "Stephen," he greeted, holding out his hand to shake. Stephen obliged and shook it back, although looking like he wanted to throw him into the water. David turned to me. "El." He smiled, as he held out his hand to me too.

Placing my hand into his, David actually looked really well. I hadn't seen him in a couple of years, since Reece was much younger and he had collected him one day from the house, but it was nice that he was turning things around - I suppose for all our sakes.

After David staring at me a little longer than he should have done, Stephen interrupted the awkwardness of mine and David's handshake.

"So, where's your sister, then, David?" he practically growled.

"In that yacht there. We've just arrived and then we saw you two. Thanks for coming tonight. It means a lot." David grinned in my direction.

Just as I was about to say it was no problem, Stephen chirped in.

"We're here for Tasha. Now shall we go in, or what?" he snapped.

"Yep. Let's do this!" Tasha beamed, seemingly more excited about this than anybody else was.

As we turned our attention to the boat, a lady emerged from inside and looked over the edge and down at us - a lady who actually took me by surprise. She was tall, with a stunning physique, wearing a long black dress, with wavy chestnut hair that was done to perfection, and deep brown eyes. She was the polar opposite of David, with his blond hair and blue eyes.

"Darcy!" David smiled up.

"Come aboard!" she shouted down to us and smiled.

David and Tasha made their way onto the yacht. As I stepped forward, I realized that Stephen wasn't walking with me. I turned to him, and noticed him frozen to the spot.

"What's up with you?" I chuckled.

"Erm, nothing. Er... I don't feel so good," Stephen replied, starting to look a pasty shade of green.

I stepped back toward him. "You're not seasick, are you?" I wondered.

"No, I've never been seasick," he bluntly replied.

"Okay, well we'll only stay for an hour... for Tasha?" I eased.

Stephen rolled his eyes. "Fine," he mumbled.

Taking his hand in mine, I led him up onto the yacht. There was a team of staff on board who smiled our way and handed us a glass of champagne on arrival, although Stephen declined and got a glass of orange juice instead. I was glad he wasn't drinking if he didn't feel too well, as I did not need him throwing up all over this yacht tonight. I wondered to myself whether it was all those awful protein shakes that he'd been drinking - I knew they'd catch up with him one day.

"Welcome!" Darcy beamed, as she led us all toward a table full of lovely food on the upper deck, overlooking the ocean.

"It's really good to see you." David smiled, as he and Darcy shared a hug. When he pulled away, he turned to Tasha. "This is Tasha, who I've told you about..." Darcy shook hands with her. "And this is Eleanor, and her husband, Stephen."

"Eleanor!" She grinned. "Now I have heard things about you..."

I blushed at the remark - this was awkward taken to another level.

"Oh, have you?" I muttered.

"All good, though!" Darcy smiled. "Don't look so worried!" She moved from around me and in the direction of Stephen, who seemed to be hiding behind me. She moved with such grace, and I always wondered how anyone did that - it was a grace that I'd never been blessed with. "Stephen, it's nice to meet you." She smiled at him, holding out her hand.

"Yeah. Nice to meet you," Stephen bluntly replied, taking her hand and limply shaking it.

Sometimes I really wished he wouldn't be so rude. I knew that he didn't feel too good and didn't want to be on this boat, but I wished he wouldn't add to the awkwardness that was already occurring on the yacht. I didn't want to be here, either, but I wasn't going to be impolite about it. It was obvious that Darcy had gone to a lot of trouble, and we didn't know her, so there was no need to assume that she would be anything like David. Darcy seemed perfectly lovely, so I was looking forward to a nice evening.

"Please, take a seat and let's eat." Darcy smiled, ushering us all over to the table full of freshly prepared food.

"This looks delicious," David commented, as we all sat down.

I looked over at Stephen, who was looking out onto the horizon, trying to ignore the fact of where he was. I gave him a little nudge with my elbow as we were all being served by the waiting staff, as if to say, 'would you please be polite'.

David and Tasha were chatting away to Darcy about Reece, and Darcy seemed to be taking great delight in hearing all about her nephew. It was nice that there was now more family about for Reece, because let's face it, in the past, family had been pretty thin on the ground.

"So how about you, Eleanor?" Darcy asked, averting her gaze to me. "What do you do?"

I swallowed the piece of fruit I had in my mouth before answering. "Er, I own a design company, Rose Designs. I don't know if you've heard of it?"

"Oh yes, I know the one. Very good... ah, the surname makes sense now!" She chuckled.

"Yes, Tasha and Stephen luckily had a beautiful surname." I grinned, looking over at Stephen who was still ignoring us all. I sighed quietly and turned back to Darcy. "So how about you... what do you do?"

"I work in law enforcement. Government security. It's really boring." She chuckled.

At that statement, Stephen turned his attention to the table. "Law enforcement?" he echoed.

Wow - I was surprised he was actually listening.

"Yes, law enforcement. It's just mainly about security. Pays well." She grinned.

At her statement, Stephen rolled his eyes and turned his attention away from the table again.

What was his problem? At least now we knew how Darcy had money - by the sounds of it she had done well. I knew Stephen wasn't impressed when anyone talked about money, so it didn't surprise me that he'd rolled his eyes at that part - although I wished he would have done it out of view of Darcy.

Darcy didn't seem bothered by it, thank goodness, as she turned back to David and Tasha to talk more about what was going on with them. David was talking about how he was a designer at a company called Jefferson's, which I'd heard of. I was glad that I was present to hear that part, as it was nice to be informed about whereabouts David was nowadays. He seemed to always know our business from Tasha, but we never heard much about him.

Tasha was jabbering on about how she wanted to go back to modeling soon, as our glasses were refilled and most of the food had been eaten. If it wasn't for Stephen, pouting in the corner like a small child, it wouldn't have been such a bad evening. Apart from the rude husband, Darcy was a lovely hostess, and I admired the fact she had risen above Stephen, and his lack of manners. I suppose working in law enforcement, she was used to people being rude, so it was a good job, really.

After a about an hour and a half of being there, I thought it would be best to make our excuses and leave Darcy, David, and Tasha to their evening. They seemed to be in great spirits catching up, and even though I wouldn't have minded staying a little longer, I thought it was best to get the man-child home.

"Darcy, thank you so much for a lovely evening." I smiled, as she walked us both out onto the harbor.

"My pleasure!" Darcy smiled back. "I hope to see you soon, Eleanor."

It didn't surprise me that she hadn't acknowledged Stephen in that statement. If somebody had been so rude to me, I wouldn't acknowledge them, either.

"Yes, thanks again. We've both got early starts tomorrow morning, so sorry we can't stay," I tried to soothe.

"It's honestly not a problem. Sleep well."

Darcy leant forward and gave me a light hug, and then smiled at Stephen, before we set back off down the harbor and toward the car. Stephen walked a few paces ahead, as I struggled to keep up behind him in my heels. It was so out of character for him, and I just couldn't see his problem at all. If anything, it should've been me that was in a mood. He had gone out of his way to ruin the evening, all because he didn't want to be there. It should've been me that was mad at him!

Getting into the passenger side myself, because Stephen had frogmarched himself straight to the driver's side, I climbed in and fastened my seatbelt. Stephen put his foot down and reversed abruptly out of the parking space, as we sped down the roads to head home.

"Would you slow down!" I yelled at him, making sure that I would be making it home to see my children.

"Sorry," he mumbled, as he realized he wasn't an F1 driver, and took his foot off the gas.

"What is wrong with you at all?" I asked, feeling fed up with his behavior at this point in time.

"Nothing," came the blunt reply.

His reply actually reminded me of Tasha, when she had first come to stay with us - she sounded exactly like that. But back then, she was an immature teenager - even though now I'd say she was quite a naive adult - but this was supposedly a grown man that I was married to, and he'd acted like a spoilt brat all night!

"It's not nothing, Stephen," I snapped. "You've been in a mood all night. I get that you didn't want to be there, but did you have to be so rude about it? The night wasn't even that bad!"

"Eleanor, just be quiet," came the reply.

Be quiet? Er, no. Nobody tells me to be quiet - not even my own husband.

"I will not be quiet!" I stated in the sternest voice I could muster. "If anything, I should be the one in a mood, because you did nothing but make a holy show of me tonight!"

"I made a show of you?" Stephen sarcastically sniggered, glancing around to quickly face me, before looking at the road again.

"Er, what is that supposed to mean? You say that like I'm the one who made a show of you! Although I was perfectly polite! I didn't sit there like some immature child! I'm not even sure what the problem was!" I huffed. "Darcy was a nice person..." I trailed off, leaning on my hand and staring out of the passenger window.

"You haven't got a clue, have you?" Stephen muttered.

I turned to face him. "A clue about what?" I sneered - he was really beginning to annoy me now.

"Nothing. Just drop it, Eleanor," he quietly muttered.

"No, I won't drop it until you tell me what is going on!" I snapped.

Stephen paused for a moment; his eyes seemingly glazing over for a second, before fixing back on the road again.

"I don't trust her," he mumbled.

"Why?" I genuinely wondered.

Stephen rolled his eyes. "No particular reason, except that she's Psycho-Sommer's sister!"

Rolling my eyes, I looked away. It was the same old argument again and again. Yes, I could see why Stephen had his reservations about her because of who she was related to, but it was really time to forgive and move on. If there was one thing that I had learnt over the years, it was that nobody could run away from their past - they had to accept it and move forward.

But another thing, when the person was trying their best, like David had been for the past three years, there was nothing worse than somebody throwing his mistakes in his face all the time. I would always remember what he had been like, but I was willing to put it behind me for my nephew's sake, and I thought Stephen was willing to do the same.

"Just get on with her for Reece's benefit. She is his aunt." I sighed, getting pretty tired of the same old argument all the time.

"Get on with her, Eleanor? I won't have to... I'm not seeing her again." He sniffed at the idea.

"I don't know, I might see her again. If she has something to do with Tasha, then she may very well appear in our lives again at some point. I thought she was quite pleasant. I couldn't see a problem. I thought she went out of her way to be a good hostess tonight, and she's done very well for herself. She said to me at the end that she would see me again soon. I just think you're being petty because of this whole David thing, that you haven't been able to drop for the past five years. Even he is trying to move on..."

"SHUT THE FUCK UP!!" Stephen raged.

Sitting upright in my seat, did I just hear that right? Wide-eyed and shocked at the outburst, I glanced over at Stephen who looked fit to burst in the driver's seat. I couldn't believe he had just spoken to me like that! I wasn't used to that with him.

Stunned, the rest of the car journey was done in total, simmering silence. Normally, if anyone had told me to shut up like that, I would've immediately snapped back, but I was in total shock at it coming from Stephen. In all the years we had been together, he'd never once spoken to me that way. Yes, we'd had our arguments and things had been said in the heat of the moment, but never like that. I didn't know what to say back, if anything, because it was completely out of character for him.

Back at the house, as soon as Stephen pulled the car up at the garages, I undid my seatbelt at top speed and hurled myself out of the car before he could even get to the passenger side - if he was even going to - and made my way into the house. I wasn't having him helping me, and he could piss off if he thought that I would be okay with the way he had spoken to me.

Once in the hallway, I took off my red heels, which felt really good, but I wasn't in the mood to savor the sweet release of my feet from the velvet confines. I could hear Stephen's footsteps making his way up to the house, so I quickly shoved the shoes to one side and made a hasty retreat up the stairs - I didn't want to speak to him.

"Eleanor..." I could hear him speak, as I dashed up the stairs to show him how pissed off I actually was.

Once in the bedroom, I grabbed hold of my nightdress and sped into the ensuite to get changed. As I was changing and brushing my teeth, I heard him enter the bedroom. Usually he'd flick on the television or something, but he was relatively silent tonight. Once ready for bed, I emerged from the bathroom to find him still dressed and sitting on the bed.

"Huh!" I huffed at him, before making my way around to my side of the bed and getting in.

"Eleanor..." he spoke again, reaching out to lean over and touch my arm.

I abruptly moved my arm away from him. "Don't touch me," I sneered, before reaching over and turning off the bedside lamp.

I could hear him shuffle about before getting changed and clambering into bed. If he thought he was going to be forgiven for that, then he was sadly mistaken.

Chapter Three - Silent Treatment

I was up and dressed early for another busy day ahead. At the moment, my days were never really laid back, and I was looking forward to in a few weeks' time when I could have some rest. As I sat with Penny and Roger in the kitchen, eating some breakfast, Stephen walked through and helped himself to some toast and his ready-made shake that was on the kitchen island, before leaving for work and not saying anything in our direction.

"What's wrong with him?" Roger half-yelped, not being used to being ignored.

"Oh, we had a fight last night. He's in a mood. It's nothing to do with you guys," I reassured.

"Men, eh?" Penny chuckled.

"Hmm..." I mumbled in agreement, sipping my coffee.

"I would take offense to that, but Ross is moody most of the time!" Roger stated, while I nearly choked on m coffee.

If anyone was moody, it was definitely Roger. I think this was a case of the pot calling the kettle black.

Penny could sense my amusement as she rose from the table. "I better get to work. I'm going to make a picnic up for Natalie and the children today!" she happily stated.

"Aw, lovely. I can't wait to have some time off soon to be able to do things like that with them." I sighed, knowing I was missing out, but as a working mom, I didn't have much choice.

"Don't worry, Chica, you are doing your best," Roger purred in his Italian accent.

"Thanks, Roger. I hope so." I sighed again, raising myself from my seat, and knowing I had to leave for work. "I'll see you guys later."

"See you later," they both called back in unison.

Chuckling to myself, I left two of my favorite people to get on with their day. I loved them both dearly, and that was something that had never changed over the years. What had changed, though, which dawned on me as I got into my car, was that whenever me and Stephen had an argument and weren't speaking to each other, I never batted an eyelid nowadays. When we were first together, I used to be devastated whenever we fell out, but I suppose that we were comfortable together now, which was never a bad thing, I suppose.

As I drove along to the Rose Designs headquarters, I realized that I had the meeting with the CEO of Brandon Corporations today. I mentally groaned at the thought of it, but it was something that had to be done. There were certain clients who would always want to see me face-to-face, as they thought they were more special if they saw the head of the company. But each person who walked through those doors were treated exactly the same way, and given an exemplary service, so it made no difference.

Getting into the building, I greeted Clarisse as she was typing away, and I did wonder whether she ever went home. I admired her work ethic, but I couldn't wait for my days off, and I owned the place! Clarisse was no quitter, and I did think how those work-yourself-into-the-ground-genes had definitely skipped me somewhere along the line. I was dedicated, yet laid back, all rolled into one.

Heading up to my office, I grabbed a coffee from the machine near my desk and sat in my seat, ready to combat the workload ahead. As I logged into the system to see what the working day would bring, my office phone rang. It was the kind of ring that was a call coming from inside the building, so I promptly answered it. It was Clarisse, telling me that I had a visitor waiting in reception for me. I wasn't expecting anyone this morning, I had no meetings planned, so I asked Clarisse to show them up to the office for me.

I sat and waited, when about a minute later, there was a knock on the door.

"Come in!" I shouted politely. The door opened and in walked someone whom I definitely hadn't seen in a while - Caroline. "Hi, Caroline!" I greeted. "Come in and take a seat."

As she walked in and closed the door behind her, I could see her security stood in the corridor of the building, which didn't shock me like it had last time they were here.

"I'm sorry to intrude upon your time, Eleanor." She smiled as she took a seat and removed her black leather gloves.

"It's not a problem. Lovely to see you again," I replied, and it was lovely to see her - this lady had saved my ass all those years ago. "Would you like a drink?" I offered.

"No, no. It's fine, thank you," she warmly replied.

I sat back down in my chair. "So, what do I owe the pleasure?" I remarked, sitting back and wondering what was with the sudden visit.

"Nothing, my dear. I thought I would call in as I was passing, and see how things were getting along." She smiled, adjusting her fur shrug.

"Very well. You've probably heard about the expansion." I grinned.

"Yes, I have. I'll be truthful, that is actually why I wanted to see you."

"Really?" I half-squeaked.

"Yes. I know this is sudden, as we haven't spoken in a while, but I would like to go into business with you," she stated.

"Er, I don't mean to sound rude..."

"I know, I know. You are not looking for any business investments at this time." She nonchalantly waved her hand in the air.

"Well, yes, but I'm also wondering, why?"

"Fair question. I also like to dip my toes in the business water."

I could see her point, but this lady had more money than you could shake a stick at - why did she want to even bother coming into business with me?

"Do you need to?" I replied, suddenly regretting the bluntness of my question.

Caroline chuckled. "You see, that's why I like you, Eleanor. You say it how it is. Believe me, I only ever go into business with people I can trust... and I know I can trust you."

"You can. That is one thing that I can assure you of. But I don't know if we need investors at this point in time." I felt guilty knocking her offer back, because if anything, our success was based on Caroline giving us all of Radar's contacts back in the day.

"You will with the expansion. I know that this expansion is something new to you, so your business acumen isn't on par right now."

I wasn't sure whether to be insulted at the statement, but if there was one thing I was aware of, it was that Caroline was not stupid.

"I'm sure my financial adviser's would inform me if I needed investors."

"Financial advisers are only there if you are managing finances. This isn't necessarily about making money for me. I have a lot of that, and where do you think that came from? Thin air? No. Myself and my family before me, have all learnt. I could be a valuable asset to you, Eleanor."

That was true. The generations of Goldsmiths that Caroline stemmed from, were renowned for having acute business brains, and that's how they had made their billions.

"It's definitely something to ponder," I thought out loud.

Caroline leant forward in her chair. "Have a think and get back to me. My offer still stands. I have always liked you. You have a spirit about you that cannot be beaten... I admire that. You remind me of myself." She smiled, standing from her chair. "We could conquer the world together."

I stood up to face her. "I will have a serious think about it. It's a very appealing offer. Thank you."

Holding my hand out to her, she shook it warmly. She walked over to the door, and I skipped ahead to open it for her. As she left, she gave me a little nod and smile of appreciation, and then exited the building - complete with her security. I went and sat back down at my desk, overwhelmed at what had been offered. Caroline Bryant, or should I say Goldsmith, is and still was, a very successful lady, and a huge part of me screamed out to not let this opportunity pass me by.

For the rest of the working day, I pondered the idea of going into business with her. There were too many perks to overlook the offer. I'd had a word with Clarisse about the situation, and she agreed that it was a fabulous opportunity. I had no reason to doubt Caroline; she had been the one person in the midst of the snakes in the grass who had been in my corner. I smirked to myself as I thought about what David would think of this if I went into business with his ex-aunt - the situation got more and more bizarre as it went along. It was another one of those situations where if I could go back and tell myself what was going to happen, I would have never believed it.

Speaking with my financial adviser's about the offer, they too agreed that Caroline would make a flawless investor. There were no concerns or red marks about Caroline. She was renowned for being business savvy, and the knowledge she would bring with her would be invaluable. She was right about one thing - I was still finding my feet in several areas of business, so I would be lucky to have her onboard.

After what seemed like hours of being at work, yet my mind being elsewhere, it was getting closer and closer to the time of my meeting with Brandon Corporations. As soon as I was able to, I pulled out a brush and lipstick from my purse to try and look more presentable - it was always important to look my best for clients. As I was brushing my hair and adding my lipstick, I heard an almighty crash outside, and looked out of the window to witness a thunderstorm hitting the area.

"*Great,*" I sarcastically thought to myself. Trust it to happen now. I would probably end up looking like a drowned rat in the meeting.

Checking the clock on my desk, it was now 6pm. It was a short drive to the restaurant, but I was willing to wait for a little while for the client. It actually would be nice to sit in a nice place and not have to think for a while. I quickly logged out of the system on my laptop and shuffled a few papers into place, picking up my purse and heading down to reception to find Clarisse still at her station.

"I'm going now!" I called out to her as I ventured along the foyer.

Clarisse looked up. "Have you seen this weather?" she asked, and yes, I had seen it - it was torrential rain and I was wondering how to avoid it.

"Yes, I'm going to have to dart inside the restaurant to avoid having a bouffant by the time I get inside." I chuckled.

"Here..." Clarisse got up and handed me an umbrella that she had behind her desk. "Take this with you."

"But don't you need it?" I asked, looking at Clarisse's slicked dark hair, which always looked perfectly refined.

"No, I'll be fine. You need it more than me, with meeting a client." She smiled as she handed it to me.

"Thanks," I replied, taking the bright red umbrella from her - well, at least the client wouldn't miss me with this and my auburn hair.

She wished me goodbye and I put on a little jog to my car. There was absolutely no point putting the umbrella up when my car was only parked a few feet away - I would've gotten absolutely drenched trying to mess around with it. Starting the engine, I headed off for the restaurant, mentally going over what we may be talking about in the meeting, and what I would say. Although I knew that whatever I had planned in my head, never usually worked out that way.

Pulling up on the street where the restaurant was situated, I noticed that there were no available parking bays directly outside. Other people weren't stupid, and had gotten to the restaurant earlier to get a spot right outside, so they didn't look like a drowned rat over dinner. I parked a few yards away, in the only spot that I'd managed to get due to a driver thankfully getting in their car and leaving. After parking up, I checked myself again in the rear view mirror to make sure that my makeup was still in place, and once satisfied, I got out with my umbrella and purse in hand.

I was so pleased that Clarisse had handed me the umbrella, as I held it in front of me to shield myself from the blast of rain that was pelting down upon me. We'd had weeks of gorgeous weather, and now this. It was sods law that it had fallen on the evening of this meeting - a meeting that I wouldn't usually have been attending.

As I neared the door to the restaurant, a gust of wind swooped under the umbrella and turned it inside out. As I fought to contain this unruly thing in my hands as it threatened to blow away, an arm reached over my head, grabbing the top of it for me and pulling it back into place so I could close it and maintain some form of control.

"Phew, thank you." I smiled as I turned to the stranger who had helped me.

"My pleasure," the voice replied.

Looking upon the stranger, we locked eyes for a moment and being honest, I couldn't take my eyes off him. He was of a tall, lean but strong stature, with short wavy hair, auburn like mine, and a well-groomed beard, and he must have been about thirty-years-old - max. He looked like someone that I would've definitely hired for a photoshoot, and his blue-green eyes twinkled back at me.

"Thanks again," I muttered, feeling my cheeks slightly heat up at staring at him for too long.

"You're welcome. Now I know why I choose not to carry one with me." He grinned, opening the door for me.

"Er, thanks again." I blushed even more, realizing that I had to stop thanking him, but I couldn't ignore him for opening the door for me.

Walking through the entrance, with the stranger following on behind me, we stopped at the front desk of the restaurant.

"May I help you?" the lady asked as she looked up at me standing there.

"Yes. I have a reservation under the name of Brandon," I replied.

"Ah yes, one of our waiters will show you to your table." She smiled, ushering for a waiter who was stood near her to take me over to where my table was.

As the waiter asked me to follow him, I turned back to the stranger:

"Nice to meet you." I smiled curtly, as he gave me a little joking salute, and I whipped myself away behind the waiter and to the table.

The waiter took me through the restaurant, past the diners who were sat talking and eating their food, and sat me at a table near to the window. It was nice in here, with white linen tables and silverware, and the client had chosen well for the meeting.

"Is this okay for you, Madam?" the waiter politely asked.

"This is lovely, thank you." I smiled, as I gave him an order for a glass of sparkling water and he walked away.

Propping my purse at the side of my place setting, I made myself comfortable in my seat. I watched as people darted left, right, and centre outside, away from the rain, and I did enjoy sitting there by myself and relaxing for a moment. Just as I was relishing in my own company, which was a rarity for me, the waiter came back with my sparkling water and placed it on the table - with someone else following him.

"There you are, Madam. Sir, may I get you a drink?" the waiter offered.

"I will have a sparkling water too, please," the voice spoke.

I looked up to witness the stranger from before, walking around the waiter and seating himself opposite me. Looking around me in a baffled fashion, I wondered whether he had mistakenly been seated with me. Did it look like we were together when I'd walked in? As he sat down, I still eyed around me - they must have made a mistake.

"I'm sorry," I whispered over to him. "I'm waiting for a client." I smiled in politeness.

"I know you are." He chuckled. "Eleanor Rose?' he replied, reaching his hand over the table.

"Yes." I gulped, feeling like an idiot, but taking his hand. "And your name is?"

He grinned at me. "Brandon Hunter. It's nice to meet you. I own Brandon Corporations."

"Oh." My face fell as I shook his hand. "I do apologize. I didn't realize that was you."

He laughed. "It's honestly not a problem. We were kind of introduced already. I wasn't sure if it was you before, but when you were seated here, I definitely knew it was."

"Right." I chuckled nervously. "So Brandon, from Brandon Corporations, I thought it might have been Hunter Corporations, as usually businesses go by the surname?" I asked, pulling myself together and taking a sip of my sparkling water.

"Brandon is a family name that several of the gentleman have had. It was agreed that it sounded a little less threatening than Hunter." He chuckled.

I laughed back. "Fair point. So you wanted to see me in person to discuss your contract?"

"Yes. I always do everything face-to-face... it takes the formalities away. I can't stand all the pompous rigmarole that goes along with business meetings." He grinned.

I smiled. "Me neither. I do like to tear down those walls when I'm given half a chance. Although I usually get one of my design team to attend these meetings, as I've had issues in the past."

"Such as?" he wondered, taking a sip of his own drink which had been brought over.

I didn't know where to start with all the crap that had gone on in my life - plus I really didn't know this man well enough to be telling him my life story.

"Oh, nothing to bore you with." I smiled.

As we were about to start talking, the waiter came over and took our order. We hadn't even had chance to look over the menu, so I ordered a chicken salad, which was usually standard in every restaurant, and Brandon ordered a steak. I actually felt really relaxed in his company, which was amazing considering I didn't know him.

We sat back after ordering, and noticed a few people getting blown by the window in the gusts of wind which were causing chaos outside.

"I'm glad to be indoors. Thank you for your help before," I thanked - again.

"You have thanked me enough." He smirked. "Wouldn't want your hair to be a mess now, would we?"

I narrowed my eyes at him - had he heard my conversation with Clarisse?

"Ha, no," I replied. "If I get my head wet, I look like a lioness!" I laughed.

"Nice hair color, by the way... we match," he remarked in referral to his own.

"We do," I spoke shyly. "Anyway, we weren't here to talk about hair color..." I chuckled, "you wanted to tell me what designs you would like from Rose?"

"Ah, yes. I have tonnes of workspaces which need designing properly. I find that grey walls and drab workspaces make for unhappy employees. I would like to change all that. My old office blocks were fine, but these new premises that we have now, well, they need a woman's touch." He grinned.

I blushed again - what the hell was wrong with me?

"I can assure you that I have a lot of wonderful male designers on my team as well." I smiled.

"I'm sure you do. Now, let's talk facts and figures."

As our meal was served up to us, we chatted about how much workspace there was and how much money, roundabout, it would take to complete. Brandon seemed to switch more into work-mode, as he listened intently to what I had to say and what the process would be. It was nice to be listened to properly by a male, as I hadn't had that pleasure from Stephen over the past couple of days.

Afterwards, Brandon sat back, removing the napkin from his lap, and leant back to observe me.

"Well, due to the great food, and even better company, I think this is a done deal." He grinned.

"Oh right. Okay... well I will get one of my team to draw up the papers for you, and have them sent over to be signed by you directly." I grinned back.

"Great. Although, as I say, I like to be more hands on with my work. When the papers are ready, with your permission, I would like to visit Rose Designs myself and have a look at how things operate there. I like to see things in action."

"By all means. We always welcome client's to come in and have a look around. You can see for yourself all of the options available, and any extra choices you maybe would like to add to your order," I offered.

"That sounds brilliant." Brandon lifted his arm and ushered for the bill to be brought over. "As productive as this evening has been, I will let you get home now. It's been an absolute pleasure to meet you, Eleanor. I will call around to

Rose Designs over the next few days. Or would you like one of my people to speak to your people to arrange something?"

"No, that's fine." I chuckled. "Call in whenever you like. We encourage people to drop by. It shows that we have nothing to hide. Plus you can always call into my office and taste the delights of my wonderful coffee machine." I laughed.

"That sounds like an offer that cannot be refused." He laughed back, placing money in the bill that had been left on the table and rising from his seat. "I better be going."

"Oh yes. I'll walk out with you if that's okay? I better be heading home," I replied as I was the next to stand from my chair.

"Of course." He smiled.

Brandon waited a moment while I made sure I had my purse, keys, and the infamous umbrella to give back to Clarisse tomorrow, and then we headed for the exit. Brandon opened the door for me as I ventured outside into the cooler, yet thankfully calmer weather than what was occurring before.

"May I?" Brandon asked, as he held out his arm for me to link. "It's only fair that I escort the lady to her car."

"That's very kind of you." I chuckled, linking my arm through his.

As we walked along to my car, I could feel the muscle of his arm and the warmth that radiated from him. It was like walking along with Stephen, when we had first gone to Paris together, and it was familiar to the point that I felt safe with him. We got to my car and Brandon released my arm from his.

"Drive safe, Eleanor." He smiled at me.

Just as I was about to reply, he looked up and around me to the buildings opposite.

"Everything okay?" I wondered, as I watched him scan the building across the street.

"Er, yes." He vaguely smiled, and after a moment, he turned his attention back to me. "I thought I recognized someone. No bother. Have a lovely night."

"Thanks, Brandon. You too," I replied, and before I could turn to my car, he darted off in the opposite direction.

Thinking that was strange, I didn't really know anything that personal about him to make a judgement. I knew what it was like in business sometimes, and I did see people from the past that I wanted to dart away from as quickly as possible. I chuckled to myself as I thought about all the people I'd darted away from in the past - it seemed that Brandon was just like me, but probably better looking, and obviously male.

Getting into my car, I headed home, ready to see whether Stephen was still in a mood with me. As I pulled up on the driveway, I noticed his car parked up, so I knew that he was home. It was now just gone 9pm, so this was late for me to be arriving back, and everybody but me would be present in the house.

Switching off the engine, I grabbed my things to make my way up to the front door. I did hate it when me and Stephen argued, probably because I knew I'd be walking into an environment that wouldn't be the best at home.

Entering through the front door, all was quiet, except for the buzz of the television coming from the living area. I placed my purse in the hallway and kicked off my shoes in my usual routine, and went to see who was in there. I knew it would be Stephen, anyway, as Natalie and the children would be upstairs by now, and Penny and Roger would have gone home.

Opening the door to the living room, lo and behold, it was Stephen, sitting back with his feet up and watching a show on the television. I mentally rolled my eyes as he didn't even acknowledge me walking through the door, and I went and sat on the recliner. I let out a sigh, as I sat back in the comfort of the chair and went over what had been talked about at the meeting with Brandon tonight.

"Good day?" Stephen mumbled in my direction.

I raised my head in surprise of having anything spoken in my direction. "Er, yes. You?" I asked.

"Fine," he bluntly answered.

Okay - well that was short and bitter.

I decided that I needed to break the ice - I couldn't stand the tension that was as thick as fog in the room.

"I did have a very interesting visit off Caroline Bryant today," I muttered.

That seemed to catch his attention and he sat up on the sofa. "What did she want?" he asked, frowning.

"She actually wants to become an investor in Rose Designs." I grinned.

"You what?!" Stephen shouted - well, it wasn't exactly what I had planned for this conversation.

"What I said. She wants to invest money into it. I think it could be a golden opportunity. She has a wealth of knowledge that she could share," I reasoned.

Stephen stood up from the sofa. "More ties to that psychotic family?!" he raged, pacing the room.

I watched on as he paced angrily backwards and forwards.

"No, she went against Bryant, if you remember. There's nothing to worry about with Caroline. Even Clarisse thinks it's a good idea."

"Pah!" he laughed. "I always thought Clarisse had a brain! Obviously not!"

"Hey!" I yelled, standing up. "Don't insult my mom like that!"

"Convenient with the whole mom thing now, isn't it?" he spat, stopping in his tracks to face me.

"What's that supposed to mean?!" I raged.

"Just now that's something else to be used against me! *You can't tell me anything about my mom, because your mom works for me,*" he mimicked in a cruel way.

"Oi!" I bellowed. "I'm not the one bringing family into anything! I was only telling you what had happened today! What the hell is wrong with you?!"

"Wrong with me?! Life was just peachy before I met you, Eleanor!" he shouted.

"What?!" I asked, bemused at yet another outburst from him.

"You heard! I'm so fed up of being dragged into mess after mess because of your *bad* decisions!" he yelled.

"What *bad* decisions?!" I shouted, totally caught off-guard with this argument.

"Where do I begin?! First it was Psycho-Sommers! Then it was Bryant! Then it was your pretend, unhinged mother, who was set to ruin you! Oh, and now it's back to Psycho-Sommer's family again!! Do you ever learn?!"

"Caroline is totally kosher! I know that by now! Plus her reputation far outweighs anything you might think! You are being totally irrational, and I don't know what has gotten into you lately!"

My blood was boiling - I'd had enough of him pushing everything onto me. I was under enough pressure without him adding to it.

"You know what?!" he raged.

"What?!" I snapped.

"You're on your own! Anything that happens now... I'm wiping my hands of it! You could cause trouble in an empty house! So now I'm going to leave you to dwell in one!"

Stephen marched to the door of the living room and huffed his way through it.

"What does that actually mean?! Jesus, Stephen, you are going to wake the children!" I shouted in a hushed tone, as he bashed around in the hallway trying to find his shoes.

"I'm going out! I need a drink! You can stay here and join forces with one of Psycho-Sommer's lot! Leave me out of it!"

He angrily stormed out of the door, slamming it behind him, as I cringed and looked up the stairs to see whether I could hear the children, and if they had been disturbed by their hot-headed father. I sighed, as I looked back into the empty living room.

Well, that went well.

Chapter Four - Alone

That night I'd gone to bed, exhausted and wondering what the hell had gotten into Stephen. I was too tired to be that bothered for long, as my days were long and my patience was wearing thin. We'd had arguments in the past, but never anything like that.

Usually it was quick to pass, but two weeks had gone by now, and Stephen was still only mumbling half-words to me - well, when he wasn't shouting at me.

He seemed to be fine with Penny, Roger, and Natalie, but I was left wondering what I'd done wrong. I wasn't having it, though - I'd been there in the past, when you were left to wonder whether you had done something without realizing it, and I didn't like living that way.

In my sheer defiance to the situation, I'd gladly taken Caroline up on her offer, which she was delighted with, and the legal wheels had been put into motion. I don't think that helped any sort of situation with Stephen, but he wasn't the one bringing the big bucks in and setting up our children's future, so he could shove his opinion. He didn't understand the business world like I did, and believe me, I had learnt valuable lessons over the years.

Although I had noticed how much Stephen was drinking lately, and that was about the only thing that concerned me. He was out almost every night, and when he wasn't out, he was avoiding me in a different room of the house. That was one of the perks of having a very large house - we didn't have to be around each other if we didn't want to be.

The more he pouted, the more I dug my heels in. I wasn't being made into some sort of victim by him. I was a fighter, and I'd survived before him, and I'd survive without him.

One night, as I sat at home reading a book and generally relaxing, Penny came through and told me that dinner was ready. I thanked her and rose from my seat, leaving my half-read book behind - the book which I had tried to finish on many occasion, but didn't seem to have much chance to. I followed her into the kitchen, to be met by an array of delights on the kitchen island.

"Miss. Eleanor, would you like me to serve up in the dining room?" she wondered, bustling about in her usual style.

"No, eating in here is great, thanks. Plus I'm not eating in there on my own." I chuckled, as I sat down at the breakfast table.

"Mr. Stephen still out, then?" Penny frowned, as she started to bring my dinner over to me.

"Yes. He'll be heading home from work now, but no doubt he'll be going straight out afterwards." I sighed.

"No doubt," Penny agreed. "Right! I have made a bit of a different meal tonight... Caramelized Onion and Cheddar Quesadilla's." She smiled, landing the plate of food in front of me.

"Sounds different." I grinned, looking on at the glorious meal that Penny had laid in front of me.

"I was using up a few ingredients that were lying around." She chuckled, and came and sat with me. "These are my daughter's favorites."

"They look amazing," I commented, as I started to dig in.

As I bit into the meal and started to chew, it tasted amazing, until I went to swallow it. I stopped chewing, as I could feel the curdle in my stomach. Looking at Penny, who was looking back at me and enjoying watching me eat her creation, I shifted awkwardly in my chair from the feeling of nausea that hit me.

"What did you say was in this again, Penny?" I asked with my mouth full.

"Caramelized onion and cheddar," she replied.

At the word 'onion', I could feel my stomach turn. I shot up from the table and raced to the downstairs bathroom, just in time for the toilet bowl to catch the remnants of my stomach, and the mouthful of food I had just had swilling in my mouth. As I heaved my guts up, after a couple of minutes my stomach managed to settle, and I felt a little better. Standing up, I composed myself and washed my hands, dabbing a bit of cool water on my face and chest.

"Is everything okay, Miss. Eleanor?" Penny called through the door.

Turning to the door, now washed up and composed, I opened it to find Penny stood there, looking like she had accidentally poisoned me.

"Yeah, I'm fine Penny, thanks." I wiped my forehead with the back of my hand and made my way back into the kitchen with her following me on behind. "That was strange," I remarked, as I sat at a bar stool, away from the table.

"Hmm, I was sure to put everything that you liked in there. No chillies or anything like that," Penny replied, racking her brain over what may have caused that reaction.

"I'm sure it's nothing you have done. I feel fine now. Ha, I remember the last time I had a bad aversion to onions, and that was when I..." I trailed off at the end, with the dawning of a memory thudding down on me.

"When what?" Penny asked, looking concerned.

"When I was pregnant with Henry," I replied in a daze.

"Oh, Miss. Eleanor... you're not? Are you?" she wondered, standing directly in front of me.

"No..." I replied in a confused manner, trying to think of when the last time me and Stephen had been together, and when my last period was - I had too much on my mind to be keeping up with such things. "Hang on, no..." My words fumbled as it was my turn to rack my memory. "I've got a test upstairs."

"Go and take it, Miss. Eleanor. If it is nothing, then it would put your mind at ease. It may just be something you ate at work today."

"True. Yeah, I'll take it before Stephen gets back. I don't want him knowing if it isn't anything." I smiled, raising myself from the bar stool and leaving Penny behind in the kitchen.

As I raced upstairs, I was suddenly aware of not needing to pee. It was typical - stage fright always got the better of me when I needed to do things such as this. I always kept a pregnancy test in the house, because me and Stephen had always planned on having a big family, so it was there in case we decided to have another baby and I could check if I was pregnant. We hadn't planned on this, though. Everything was so hectic lately, but then again, when did anything ever run smoothly in this house?

Venturing into the ensuite, I rifled around in the bathroom cabinet. Once I located the test, I quickly stripped it of its wrapper and sat on the lavatory, willing myself to go. After a while, my bladder engaged with my brain and I did what had to be done on the stick. Replacing the cap at the tip of the test, I washed my hands, before wandering back out into the bedroom and finding the clock on the bedside cabinet. After watching three minutes of my life ebb away from me, I turned the test stick over. Peeping up at me, was indeed, two blue lines - I was pregnant.

What I felt in that moment, I don't know. After having three children, it wasn't a massive shock anymore, but I did feel a bit surprised, in a nice way. Although unplanned, I was pleased to be having a little life growing inside of me. It always felt strange in a blessed kind of way.

Making my way to the top of the stairs to go and show Penny the test, I heard the front door click open. Knowing it was Stephen, I wondered how I was going to tell him the news - especially with the way things were between us at the moment. I watched from the top of the staircase, as he placed his work bag down and walked through to where Penny was. There was no time like the present to let him know.

Venturing downstairs, I kept the test behind my back, as I went back into the kitchen to find Stephen happily chatting away with Penny. That was another thing that annoyed me with him – the way he was as nice as pie to other people, yet was treating me like some kind of leper - still with no idea as to what I had done wrong.

"Miss. Eleanor, there you are!" Penny greeted, as I walked back in.

Stephen, who was sat down at the kitchen island, looked at me and then stood up as if to leave because I had entered the room. Penny could sense the friction in the air as he was about to leave, so she made an excuse that she had cleaning to do in another room, and left us in peace. I smiled at her as she walked past me, to thank her for being tactful.

"I'm going, too," Stephen mumbled, as he went to walk past me.

"Stephen," I replied, gently holding onto his arm as he walked by me, "I really have to talk to you."

"Can't it wait?" he snapped. "I'm going out with Mark tonight."

"No, it can't," I impatiently replied.

Stephen sighed like a teenager who had been told he was grounded. "What is it, then?"

I sighed myself and looked down at the floor, before looking up again and meeting his eyeline.

"This," I stated, retrieving the stick from behind my back and handing it to him. "I'm pregnant."

"Who's is it?" he sarcastically replied.

I looked upon him in sheer horror at being asked that.

"Are you fucking serious?!" I yelled.

He sighed, his broad shoulders slumping. "Okay, I'm sorry."

"No, I'm not having it! How dare you come out with something like that when I have just told you that I'm having OUR baby!" I fumed.

"Yeah, I shouldn't have said that," he replied, admitting defeat.

"No, you shouldn't have. I don't recognize you anymore!" I yelled, feeling upset and depleted at the mess my marriage was in - for reasons unknown to me.

"Eleanor, I..." Stephen reached out to place his hand on my arm.

"Get off!" I sharply replied, moving away from him. "Just go out and get drunk... that seems to be all you are good for!" I stormed, hastily walking out of the kitchen and going back upstairs to the bedroom.

I slammed the bedroom door behind me in a fit of rage - how dare he be like that with me! I would, I could, understand if it was for a valid reason, but I didn't know why he was behaving that way! He hadn't been near me in weeks - I was surprised that we'd actually managed to conceive a baby! Yet when I'd told him, he'd replied with that! I was seething when I thought about him. I was right about one thing - I didn't recognize him one bit.

As I sat on the bed, the tears streamed down my face. Things were getting worse between us, and I never thought anything would end up like this between me and him. He had always been my hero, but now he was acting like my enemy. As the tears fell, I heard the distant sound of the front door slamming shut - he'd obviously gone out again. I never even knew where he was going, and he usually used to tell me those things. He hadn't been near me in weeks, he was out drinking all the time, and doing goodness-knows-what else.

Laying myself down on the bed, I sobbed my heart out. In the past, when I had found out I was expecting, it had been filled with love and jubilation. Now, it was filled with resentment and bitterness. I loved Stephen, but at the moment I didn't like him at all.

In that moment, as I lay down and sobbed, I realized that the one emotion that overtook all others was loneliness. Even in the days before Stephen, I had never felt this lonely. How could I be married, yet feel like that as well? Usually he was not only my husband, but my companion, my lover, and yet I was left in a pit of confusion and not knowing what was going to happen next.

Drying my tears, knowing full well that pregnancy hormones probably weren't helping, I decided that one thing was for certain - I wasn't letting any man make me feel that way. Tomorrow, I would get up, dress up, and make sure he knew what he was losing out on.

IN THE MORNING, I GOT up a little earlier than usual. I was determined that Stephen's behavior was not going to get me down any longer. I was fed up with being the villain of the piece, and I had better things to do than mope over him. I quickly called through to my local doctors, as I had to make sure that I had a midwife and everything else set up. I didn't need Stephen for any of this, and I would carry on with my life as normal.

I had Roger do my hair and makeup, and specifically requested that he slick my hair back into a modern bun, and give me a more dramatic look - it was time to show the world what I was made of. Roger was thrilled to pieces with me wanting to try out a new style, and happily obliged. When I looked in the mirror, I looked like a 1950s movie siren, and I loved it. It was different for me, but I looked like a glamorous, yet strong woman, who could handle anything thrown her way.

In a different routine, I called through to Clarisse, and told her that I would be a bit late to the office, as I was going to do a little retail therapy. As much as shopping wasn't exactly a thrilling prospect, sometimes retail therapy was what was in order, and I wanted to treat myself nicely - after Stephen treating me like dirt.

Bypassing Stephen in the hallway, I strode along in my six-inch heels - which really wasn't like me. With my designer clothes on and makeup and hair done to perfection, I was ready to take on the world. I could see Stephen's eyes pop a little as I walked past him, but I wasn't about to be saying anything to that idiot. He could stew in his own juices, and watch on as the woman he had married would be saying to him, in a roundabout way, to go and screw himself.

Shouting a goodbye back to Penny and Roger, who were watching on from the entrance of the kitchen, I wandered confidently out of the house and to my car. Sitting in the driver's seat, I dropped my guard down a little bit as I could feel a slight queasiness from morning sickness, which luckily soon ebbed away.

Driving in six-inch heels was no easy feat, and I wished I would have packed some flats in the car, but hindsight was always wonderful. Getting to the mall, I had a wander around, splurging on expensive items that I didn't usually bother with, but I thought I may as well buy, just because I could. As I carried my various shopping bags back to my car, it dawned on me what I was doing. I didn't mind a new look and feeling more confident, but I was trying to fill a void of emptiness with designer items, and frankly, it wasn't working.

Deciding that retail therapy wasn't cutting it, I thought that I better had get to work. It hadn't really dawned on me until today about how empty I actually felt. Money definitely couldn't buy happiness, as I had plenty of it, and my marriage was quickly turning into the pits, with no amount of money being able to save it.

Pulling into Rose Designs, I also realized that I didn't mind entering this building - it was the only building that was welcoming. At home, Penny and Roger were fantastic, and thankfully Natalie was great with the children, but since Stephen had gone all dramatic on me, I never felt welcomed with him at all. At one point in time, he had been my home, and my heart, but now he was fast becoming a stranger to me. Getting into the reception area, Clarisse looked up from her laptop to greet me again.

"Eleanor! Wow, you look fantastic!" She smiled as she stood up from her seat.

"Thanks." I smiled in appreciation of the compliment, but I didn't feel that fantastic inside.

"You have a visitor in your office. I've given him a coffee and he's waiting for you."

"Who is?" I wondered.

"Oh yes, sorry... where is my mind today?" Clarisse chuckled. "Brandon Hunter."

"Oh, lovely. Thanks, Mom." I smiled - she wasn't the only one with her mind elsewhere at the moment.

Heading straight up to my office, I'd actually forgotten that Brandon had told me he wanted to visit the place. But with his order impending, I suppose it only made sense that he would visit now to see how we did things at Rose. I opened the door to my office and found him stood at the window, looking out onto the view and holding his coffee.

"Hi, Brandon," I greeted, as I removed my coat and hung it next to the door.

He turned around to face me. "Wow, you look stunning. Hi, Eleanor." He smiled.

Still unable to ebb the blood flow to my cheeks, I smiled his way and then went and sat in my seat at my desk.

"So, you're here today for a visit?" I asked.

"Yes, if that's okay with you. I would've visited sooner, but work has kept me very busy." He grinned.

"No problem. I understand how hectic things can get." I stood back up. "Come on, I'll show you around now."

Realizing that this wasn't the best footwear after all, I showed Brandon around the various departments - trying not to let the pain of my feet blistering show on my face. Brandon seemed to be interested in every segment of the company, and he thoroughly enjoyed conversing with several members of staff who were keen to show off their work.

"You have an amazing team," Brandon remarked on the way back up to my office.

"Thank you. I do value them a lot. They're good people." I smiled.

"You can tell. When a workplace is happy, it shows. Which is why I am in need of your services to accomplish the same vibe."

"You're in the right place. Now, is there anything else you would like to see while you're here?" I wondered as I opened up the door to my office to let us both back in. We stepped inside and I closed the door behind us.

"Well, I hope you don't find me rude when I ask this..." He paused, stopping in the middle of my office and turning to me. "I would like to take you for a drink after work... to say thank you."

"Oh, erm... er..." I mumbled.

"Listen, I understand that you're married, and it would be completely pla-tonic. Just as friends, and to say thank you for today." He smiled warmly.

"Er, yeah okay... but I can't drink at the moment."

"Oh, any reason why not?" he asked.

Another thing that I didn't know him well enough for, to be telling him.

"No, it's just that I'm busy at the moment, so have cut back. I like to have a clear head in the morning as well." I chuckled, covering up the real reason.

"Fair enough. Sparkling water it is then." He winked. "But you can go home first and get ready. I'll get a car to come and collect you from your house and then take you back after."

"Oh, well, that's very kind of you. I could always get a car myself, though, if it's too much trouble."

"Not at all!" he protested. "I like to know that any ladies around me are looked after. I'll pick you up at 8pm, and we'll go to Bar Tab." He smiled, making his way to the door. Just as I was about to stand and show him out, he ushered for me to sit back down. "You stay there," he spoke. "I'll show myself out."

Sitting back, I gave him a smile of appreciation and told him I would see him later. I watched Brandon as he left; he was a stunning man, and I suppose he could get any ladies that he wanted, so I should've been flattered that he wanted to take me out. I understood that it wasn't a date, but still, it was nice to feel a little wanted these days.

As I sat there, a pang of guilt hit the pit of my belly, as I thought about Stephen. I quickly shoved the thought to one side on the pretence that he didn't care about gallivanting about with goodness-knows-who while I was sat at home, so it would wipe his eye if I did it for a change. I was actually a bit excited when I thought about it. It would be nice to spend some time with a handsome man who actually wanted to speak to me.

THAT EVENING, I TOLD Penny my plans as she was making dinner - and before Stephen got home - and asked Roger to stick around for dinner and fix up my makeup and hair again for me. We sat around the table chatting, as Natalie brought the children in to see me, so I could wish them a good night. One-by-one, I held the children close, as I nuzzled into them and gave them each a kiss. I did miss them, but I knew that soon I would have more time with them, although in a few months they would have another brother or sister joining them.

I hadn't told Natalie about me having another baby just yet, as I wasn't sure if she could take any more children on. Also, with it being early days, I wanted to bide my time with giving out the news to the people closest to us. Plus with the mood Stephen had been in, I was trying to go about life as normal without adding baby news to the mix.

The only people I had confided in about my pregnancy was Penny and Roger, and they were both thrilled for me. It was nice to have a couple of very close friends aware of it, and share in the joy that a baby did bring, but it was a pity that it wasn't my husband sharing in it right now.

"Are you sure you want to be going out tonight?" Penny warned, as I sat there eating my meal.

"Of course, why not?" I wondered, with my mouth half-full.

"Because, Chica, you are in a very delicate position. Plus wid de way dat Stephen is behaving..." Roger chipped in.

"I don't care about him! He does whatever he wants!" I protested. "Anyway, I'm going out with a business associate... a friend... it's not a date!" I chuckled.

"Are you sure?" Penny wondered. "Some men find the forbidden fruit the sweetest." She chuckled.

"I'm sure." I chuckled back. "Brandon is a nice guy, and it's purely platonic."

"Chica, sometimes the ways of the male variety is totally out of your understanding!" Roger laughed.

"Maybe so, but no matter whether I am married or not, I'm having a baby, and that would be a little bit weird." I frowned.

"True, true!" Roger agreed. "Anyway, let's get you looking gorgeous, Chica! He will be here soon to collect you!" He smiled.

It was nice that Penny and Roger understood me. It was also nice to be looked at like sometimes I wasn't just a wife and a mother, but I was also a woman.

Gulping down the last of my onion-free meal, I went and joined Roger in the salon. The usual frenzy of hair and makeup began, as he let my auburn locks loose for tonight and curled them to perfection. When he had finished, I dashed up to my bedroom, and decided that tonight I would wear my little black dress - perfect for any occasion. I was really looking forward to tonight, as it had been ages since I'd had a nice night out with a friend, and if that friend happened to be a handsome young man, then great!

Heading back downstairs and noting the glow of headlights flash across the glass panes of the front door, I knew that Brandon had arrived. Just as I got to the bottom of the staircase, Stephen walked through the front door, curiously eyeing the black, shiny car on the driveway. He turned back into the house and saw me walking towards the door. He looked me up and down, and a slight frown crossed his expression.

"Where are you going?" he asked - which was possibly the longest sentence he'd spoken in my direction in ages.

"Out," I bluntly replied, grabbing my black purse from on top of the cabinet next to the door.

As I opened the front door wide, Brandon was stood there, reaching out as if just about to knock.

"Hi, Eleanor." Brandon smiled, looking dashing in a lovely suit, and eyeing the situation of me and Stephen stood awkwardly together.

"Hi, Brandon." I smiled back at him.

"Who the hell are you?" Stephen sneered.

I whirled round to face Stephen. "Don't be so rude." I turned back to Brandon. "Brandon, this is my husband, Stephen. Stephen..." I reluctantly turned back to him, "this is a business associate of mine, Brandon."

"Nice to meet you," Brandon replied, holding his hand out for Stephen to shake.

Stephen shook his hand, and I could see the tug of war going on between both men - there seemed to be a mini fight of who had the strongest handshake.

"Right, let's go." I motioned to Brandon, who was looking Stephen dead in the eyes.

"Of course. I'll wait for you in the car." He smiled, before shooting a glance at Stephen, and walking back down the steps.

Stephen took hold of my arm to stop me from leaving. "What do you think you are doing?" he hissed.

I looked him in the face. "Going out with a business contact. You heard me introduce him. Which, let's face it, has been more of an introduction than I have gotten recently, with you pissing off out left, right and centre, with good-ness-knows-who."

He let go of my arm. "I don't trust him," he quietly muttered toward me.

"You never trust anyone, Stephen. You know your own tricks best, so try practising what you preach." Just as I went to step out of the house, I turned back to look at him again. "Another thing, as you say, none of this has anything to do with you anymore," I snapped, pulling the front door closed behind me and leaving him stood in the hallway.

I could feel the sadness tug on my chest as I walked away from him. I felt guilty for behaving that way, but perhaps a taste of his own medicine would make him see sense. Getting to the bottom of the steps, the driver was stood by the car, holding the door open and waiting for me to get in. As I ducked down, I could see Brandon sat on the other side, smiling at me.

"Everything okay?" he asked, as I slipped into the seat next to him.

"Yes, everything is fine," I lied. "Shall we go?"

"Of course," he replied, as he motioned for the chauffeur to drive away.

As I glanced back at the house, I could see the silhouette of Stephen standing behind the glass pane of the door, and my heart broke a tiny bit. As much as I wanted to give him a taste of his own medicine, the state we were in did not make me feel good at all.

There wasn't much time to dwell on it though, as Brandon animatedly spoke about upcoming projects and told me about how excited he was to see what Rose Designs was going to do for him. Before I knew it, we pulled up at Bar Tab, and the car stopped right outside. The driver opened the door for us, and Brandon got out first, then held my hand to help me out. I smiled and thanked him, as he put his arm out for me to link and we went inside together. The place was very glitzy, and the atmosphere was buzzing with the richest clientele, drinking, and laughing together.

We were seated at a booth, and Brandon ordered a beer for himself and a virgin cocktail for me.

"I couldn't have you coming out with me, and not at least having a pretend drink." He smiled as he handed it to me.

"Thanks." I laughed. "I quite like these anyway."

We sipped our drinks and chatted some more about work. It was so nice to be out of the house for a while and not wondering where Stephen was all the time.

"So, what do you like to do in your spare time?" Brandon asked, after he was telling me about his latest scuba diving holiday.

"I'm not as adventurous as you." I chuckled. "Life is pretty full on at home and what not. Having three children will make things that way."

"Aw, you've got kids?" he asked, sipping his drink.

"Yes, twins and a boy. They keep us all busy. I adore them." I smiled, recalling their beautiful faces.

"You can tell. Your eyes light up when you talk about them," Brandon commented sweetly.

"Do they really? I wouldn't know." I laughed.

"Yeah, they do. I love kids. Coming from a small family, I never had much interaction with little ones, but some of my friends are married and have kids, and I love being Uncle Brandon to them."

"Aw, that's nice. I have a sister, Michelle, but I don't really hear from her as much nowadays. Her and her husband, Pete, they have a holiday home in Europe, and she spends most of her time there. She'll text and call, and it's always nice to hear from her, but they haven't got any kids yet."

"What about your husband's side?" Brandon wondered.

"He has a sister called Tasha. Tasha has a little boy, Reece, who's three. He's a sweetheart." I grinned.

"Ah right, is she not with anyone?"

"No, not at the moment. Well, I think she's hooking up with the father of her baby, but they're not together, together... if you know what I mean." I chuckled.

"Sounds interesting." He smiled, looking out onto the crowded dancefloor.

"Hmm, it is... although if we become friends, you'll soon find out how complex my life really is." I laughed.

Brandon laughed back. "What's life without a little drama, eh?"

"I wouldn't mind a little... just not a lot." I sniggered.

"Would you like to dance?" he offered.

"Really? You dance?" I eyed.

"Yeah. I've been known to have moves." He laughed.

"Okay, let's go."

Brandon stood up and took my hand to lead me onto the dancefloor. It was busy, but luckily people just seemed to be having a good time, and it was great to be a part of it. Brandon whirled me around by my arm to face him, as we both started bopping along to the music that was playing. He wasn't lying, he really did have rhythm, and we laughed and joked as he took my hands and started moving me along to the beat of the next few songs ahead.

I actually felt great, and really carefree, as we danced and laughed together. Brandon was not only very handsome, but he was good fun, too. There was definitely a connection between us, although the warnings from Penny and Roger rang out in my mind. But I wasn't sure whether the connection between us was of a romantic nature. I wasn't looking to pursue anything anyway, as I was obviously still married. I loved Stephen, even for all of his hot-headed flaws, and I was hoping that the situation between us, given time, would resolve itself.

After what seemed like an eternity of dancing, we sat back down at the booth, feeling puffed out and mildly sweaty.

"That was good fun!" I smiled, shouting over the music which seemed to have gotten louder.

"Don't sound too surprised! I'm a hoot!" Brandon joked.

I laughed back. His sense of humor was wicked, and I found myself drawn to that. I still couldn't work him out, because men were generally after one thing, but he hadn't put a foot out of place with me, and I was thankful he was a real gentleman. I suppose it was early days in our friendship, though, and I was aware to watch out for anything like that in future.

A couple of hours later, feeling good and after more great conversation, we decided it would be best to head back home. It was now midnight, and considering I was supposed to be in work first thing in the morning, I knew I had to get some rest.

Pulling back up at the house, I turned to Brandon. "Thanks so much for tonight, I had a really nice time," I beamed.

"My pleasure. It's been great to spend some time with you. Here, I'll walk you to your door."

Just as I was about to say that it was no problem and I'd walk myself, Brandon shot out of the car before the chauffeur could even attempt to open the door, and was at the passenger side helping me out.

"There's really no need." I chuckled, as I got myself out of the vehicle, using Brandon's hand for leverage.

"Oh, there is. I know you're safe when I get you to the door." He smiled, as we walked together up the steps.

"Thanks again." I smiled back, looking into his lovely turquoise eyes.

"You're always welcome, Eleanor. Sleep well." Brandon nodded curtly and then ventured back down the front steps to get back in the car.

Making my way into the house, I waved him off as I stood in the doorway. He wound the window down and waved back at me as the car was driven away, and I felt happier and more content than I had done in weeks.

Closing the front door, I slipped off my shoes, and noticed that the living room light was on through the gap at the bottom of the door frame. Thinking it was strange that the light was left on, I went to investigate who was in there. I opened the door to find Stephen sat on the sofa, with his duffle bag next to him.

"What are you doing?" I asked, as I eyed him sat there in the complete silence of the room.

"I was waiting for you. I thought it would be better than leaving a note or a text message."

I knew what he meant - he was leaving me.

"You're leaving?" I wondered.

"Yes. I think it's best that we have some time apart."

"For how long?" came my next question.

"I don't know. I don't know whether it should be a permanent thing."

I felt numb. I didn't know whether I was angry, sad, or plain pissed off.

"What's going on with you? You have been off with me for weeks, and I have racked my brain, but I can't think what I've done wrong," I sadly replied.

"You haven't done anything wrong," he answered. "Well, except for tonight."

"Meaning?"

Stephen stood up from the sofa. "Meaning, you are pregnant with our child, and you are gallivanting around town with some guy who isn't your husband!" he snapped.

"Ha, you're one to talk! You have done nothing but gallivant around! Who knows who with?! At least you have acknowledged I'm having a baby, and believe it or not, Stephen, I have to take the baby everywhere with me, so I'm very careful about who I'm with and what I do. Must be nice when you don't have the responsibility of carrying a child in your body."

Stephen lowered his head. "I'm sorry," he muttered.

"For what? Being a complete asshole, or for treating me like one?" I snapped back. "Do you not love me anymore?"

Stephen looked up at me with his expression softening. He slowly edged toward me, and placed a hand on my arm.

"Of course I do. I don't think that will ever change. But we can't be together... I'm not the person who you thought I was."

"Oh, it's the, 'it's not you, it's me' lame excuse. Cut the crap, Stephen, we've been together for years... I think I do know who you are." I rolled my eyes with impatience at his words.

"Okay, well I'm not sure I know myself anymore," he corrected.

I shook my head in confusion. "You keep talking in riddles. What's changed? Your attitude has changed over the past few weeks, and I don't know why." I reached out to him, and cupped his face with my hand. "I do love you, and I would like to fix this. I thought we were stronger than this. We've been through so much."

His chocolate eyes fixed in mine, settling comfortably into my own irises and softening at my words. For a brief moment, I could see the old Stephen peeping back at me - the man that I absolutely adored, and had always done his best to look after me and keep me safe.

He reached forward and our lips touched. It felt so good to feel him near me. Our kiss grew more passionate as we wrapped our arms around each other, and he held me tightly against him. Just as it was getting to the stage of wanting to rip each other's clothes off, he quickly stepped back, releasing me from his arms as I stood there breathlessly.

"I can't do this," he panted, running his hands through his hair.

"What do you mean, you can't do this? I'm your wife, Stephen!" I yelled.

"I know. I just... I... I've got to go. I'll be in touch." Stephen whipped around, grabbing his bag and hastily making his way to the door.

I called him back as he was leaving, but it was no use. He left me stood there alone in the living room, not knowing whether I was coming or going with him.

As I stood there, replaying what had just happened in my mind, one part of our conversation stuck in my head. It was the part about how he said he couldn't do this with me, and me saying that he could because I was his wife. That conversation had happened to me before, but in reverse. It had happened that day when David had kissed me when I had gotten back from my Paris trip with Stephen.

I knew it there and then. One thing was very clear...

He'd met someone else.

Chapter Five - Nature's Way

A couple of days passed, and I went about my business as per usual. Work was busy, but it was a good distraction in terms of keeping my mind off Stephen. While I did feel upset about it, I couldn't shake the feeling of being baffled by it all. He said that he didn't know himself anymore - what did that even mean?

No matter how much I thought over it, it was no use. I'd come to the conclusion that it was just an excuse, and that he had obviously met someone else, but was too spineless to admit it to me. I would never have thought of Stephen as spineless, and I even surprised myself to be describing him that way, but he was. He'd walked out on me and our children, and I think I was still in denial about the reality of the situation.

I had to keep moving forward. I hadn't heard from him since the night he had left. Maybe he had changed? Because he never went a day without at least making contact with his children, yet there had been nothing heard from him. I should have been concerned about the disappearing act, but from the way he had been acting lately, I knew that it was best to give him his space and then see what came next.

Getting home that evening, I kicked off my shoes and wandered into the living room to relax. My back had been aching all day, and I knew it was best to keep off my feet. I'd had a late lunch at work, so I didn't even feel hungry. I was exhausted, and I really wanted to get some sleep. After sitting on the sofa and willing myself to move, I bypassed Penny, who was milling around and about, and went straight up to bed. It had gone 7pm - my working days seemed to be getting longer - so the children were in bed, and I knew that it was a good idea to get some much needed rest.

Entering the bedroom, I undressed into my night clothes and got into bed. I felt queasy, and while I was used to that feeling by now, my body ached, and I desperately wanted to relax. I lay down in bed and let the lull of sleep take me away. The bed was lovely and cushy, and I realized that I had been overworking myself way too much.

As I lay in a deep dream state, dreaming of something occurring in my life that was muddled beyond belief, I awoke to a sharp pain in the pit of my stomach. It jolted me awake, and I sat upright in the bed, still half-asleep. All of a sudden, an urge to use the bathroom hit, so I climbed out of bed and went into the ensuite. I sat on the lavatory and looked down. There, on my underwear, was blood.

"No..." I whispered to myself, as I looked down and wondered whether I was still dreaming.

Wiping myself, there was more blood on the toilet paper, and I knew that this was not good. Carefully, I got up from the lavatory and walked back into the bedroom to lie back on the bed. Grabbing my cell, I called the emergency doctors - I wasn't sure whether to go to the hospital or not. I didn't want to be driving, and with Stephen not here, there was nobody else I could ask. I checked the time and it was 11pm - Penny and Roger would be at home, and there was only Natalie with the children in the house.

A lady answered on the other end of the line, and I told her what was happening. She informed me that she would call me back with some advice as to what to do - if anything - and I was glad to be getting some sort of assistance. The period cramps ripped through my stomach, and, call it intuition, but I knew what was happening.

Using some feminine products to stop myself from bleeding all over the bed, several minutes later, a doctor called me back. The doctor asked me how far I was, and I told him I was a few weeks along. As I knew deep down already, the doctor told me that I was suffering a miscarriage, and to try and rest. He told me that there was nothing that they could do, and I would have to let nature take its course. His only advice was that I should rest as much as possible.

I got off the phone, feeling like I was still half-asleep, and that this was some sort of nightmare. I could feel the aches of the cramps in my stomach, and the welling of tears in my eyes. Lifting my cell again, I decided that I had to speak to Stephen - I couldn't believe this was happening. I dialed his number and it rang, and rang, and rang, until eventually it went to voicemail.

As my anger grew, so did the aches in my stomach, and that in turn made things worse. I knew that this was a combination of too much work, and due to the stress of his behavior, which was why it was happening. I also knew that these things just happened, but a large part of me held him accountable for it.

And where was he now? Probably out drinking with his friends, or with another woman - freaking brilliant.

Lying there, I cried as I went through it alone. Completely alone and abandoned. I could feel the turmoil inside, and I felt so guilty when I thought about how this baby would've been better off out of this mess. But no, this baby would have been as loved as Madison, Mason, and Henry, and I would not be allowing Stephen's cracked behavior to make me feel any differently.

I had to have someone with me, and I knew that the best person to call would be my mom. Once again, I grabbed my cell and pulled up Clarisse's number. After a couple of rings, she answered, and I was so thankful that she wasn't ignoring me, like some other people I could mention.

"Eleanor?" she asked, as I couldn't speak through the tears that were streaming.

"Mom..." I sniffled, trying to ebb away the tears.

"What's wrong?" she asked, sounding concerned on the other end of the line.

"Mom, could you come over? I really need you," I whimpered.

"Of course. I'm on my way." And with that, she was gone.

I lay back and let the grief wash over me. I was heartbroken at what was happening, and a whirl of thoughts were going through my mind. What felt like moments later, I could hear her coming up the stairs. She knocked on the door, and I shouted for her to come in.

"Eleanor!" she gasped, noting me lying in tears on the bed. "I looked for you all over the house! What's going on?"

"Oh, Mom!" I burst into tears again, as she came over to the bed and held me in her arms.

As she sat there, gently rocking me to try and soothe my pain, she pulled slightly away from me and asked me what was wrong. I told her about the miscarriage and how Stephen had left me; skirting over a lot of things because I didn't want to rake through it all.

"Oh, sweetheart," she soothed as she pulled me in closer - the scent of her perfume being a huge comfort to me.

She didn't say anything else as we sat and hugged each other, and I cried until I couldn't produce anymore tears. I hadn't even realized that I'd fallen asleep after what seemed like an age of being cradled in her arms, and the next thing I knew, I was waking up in the morning.

For a second, I opened my eyes and had forgotten. For that brief moment, everything was perfectly normal - and then reality hit. It hit in the pit of my stomach, and I carefully raised myself out of bed.

"What are you doing?" came the voice of Clarisse, as she dashed into the room with a breakfast tray.

"I want to get up," I mumbled, as I carefully propped myself on the edge of the bed.

"You need to rest, sweetheart." She smiled gently, as she lay the breakfast tray next to me.

"Have you been here all night?" I wondered, as I took a slice of toast off the plate and bit the corner off, not feeling hungry but knowing I had to eat something.

"Yes. I slept in the bed next to you in case you woke in the night. Then I got up early, and I grabbed a few breakfast bits and pieces with Penny's help, to bring up to you."

"Did Penny wonder why you were here?" I croaked, unable to digest the piece of toast.

"She was surprised, but I said that you needed me last night. I didn't tell her anything. I didn't know whether she knew or not," she softly explained.

"She knew I was pregnant," I replied sadly, wondering where it had all gone so wrong.

Clarisse moved closer to me and put her arm around my shoulders. "Do you want to get more rest, darling?" she asked.

"No, I want to get up and showered. There's no point in resting... it's not like anything can be done about it." I unhappily sighed.

"You need to take it easy, and let yourself heal. Just one day at a time, yeah? And at least it's Saturday, so you don't have to worry about work. Does Stephen know what's happened?"

"I tried calling him, but he's ignoring my calls. I don't want to speak to him now, anyway. I'm angry at him, but I'm angrier with myself."

"How so?" Clarisse gently asked.

"Because if I would have taken it easy, this wouldn't have happened. I've been pushing myself, and making out I was this strong, capable woman, when I should have had my feet up. Plus I was letting Stephen's stupid behavior get to me. My stress levels have been through the roof." The tears started trickling down my cheeks again.

"Hey, come on. Stop blaming yourself. This is *not* your fault. Sometimes things like this happen, and it's nature's way of it not being the right time. There's so many reasons why you could have had a miscarriage, and you are not to be beating yourself up about it. Okay?" Clarisse looked sterner toward me, and I think it was the first time that I had been kind of told off by her - in a nice way.

"Thanks so much for being here." I smiled through the tears.

"Anytime, sweetheart. I love you, and I will always be here for you."

"I love you, Mom."

THE REST OF THE DAY was spent carefully manoeuvring around the house. Clarisse was right about one thing; I was still healing and I could feel it. I was at a loss, but at the same time, I had an inner strength that I was not going to let this happen again. I wasn't sure whether I was hurting more about the baby, or about the fact that Stephen wasn't with me. It was a double-edged sword, and I knew that I was going to have to strengthen up and deal with it.

As much as a large part of me pined for the loss of the little life that had been briefly growing inside of me, the only thing I was remotely thankful for, was that it was very early days when it had happened. My heart went out to anyone who had to go through it at a later stage.

Calling the doctors again, I decided that I wanted an appointment to be checked over. The doctor confirmed to me that I had indeed suffered a miscarriage, and told me to take it as easy as possible until the bleeding subsided.

I wept more tears and went through the emotional throws that the next few days threw at me, and luckily Clarisse was an absolute blessing. Penny and Roger were informed, and I was glad for their support. They were very sensitive about such a subject, and promised that it would stay within the four walls. I was relieved that I hadn't told anyone else, because I couldn't bear to have to explain to anyone else about what had happened.

Eventually I went back to work, and whilst a part of me did feel guilty about having to get on with my life knowing that I wasn't going to be bringing a little one into the world in less than nine months' time, I knew I had to do it. I'd cried my tears, I was still ebbing my way out of the grief, but I had to be strong and overcome this for my own sake. Clarisse was right; there was no use in beating myself up over it all the time. It wasn't solving anything.

The only problem I really had, was facing Jeanie at work. I'd spent my time avoiding her, as I didn't want to speak to her about Stephen. I'd asked Clarisse to let her know that Stephen had left me, and that I didn't know where he was, but I knew that he was still in touch with Jeanie, otherwise she would have been the first to approach me with her concern if she hadn't have heard from him. I didn't blame Jeanie for anything, as she was caught between the devil and the deep blue sea; working for me whilst her son had walked out on his marriage. But what could any of us really do about this situation? It was time to suck it up, and not let him hurt me again. He obviously didn't care what was going on at home, and with Jeanie not knowing about the baby in the first place, I could be left in peace.

As the days merged into one in a work-filled blur, the expansion was coming to completion, and the lawyers were in the midst of bringing Caroline into the business - the dust was finally starting to settle. I'd asked my lawyer, Mr. Franks, to deal with the legal side of the business dealings with Caroline, and he was as amazing as ever, taking as much of the flack away from me as possible. Apart from home-life, business was running amazingly well, and I was glad about that. I wasn't sure how I would've dealt with that going ass up along with everything else.

I had decided, much to Clarisse's relief, to take a few days off. She kept telling me that I was working too hard, and after what had happened, I was inclined to agree. I now needed a respite more than ever, so while everything was going great at work, I forced myself to take a few days off to relax at home and recuperate.

While that was a good idea in theory, I spent more time with the children, and whilst I adored them, they were not what I would call relaxing. They ran rings around me, and I wondered how Natalie did this almost twenty-four-seven. As I watched them play, it did put a little sting in my chest when I thought about the baby, but I was healing nicely, and I knew I couldn't carry on torturing myself any longer. My body was back to normal now, and it was time to get my mind in the same position - for my children's sake, more than anyone else. Seeing their mother with tears in her eyes and not knowing what was wrong, was doing nothing for their own stability.

After oodles of playing and trying to split up a couple of arguments between the twins, Natalie told me that she would take them out to a playgroup for a couple of hours to let them blow off steam. They had bundles of energy, and while school was out for a break, they needed an outlet for it.

Sitting myself down in the living room, I put my feet up in order to read the book that I'd tried to finish on many occasion, when I received a buzz of a text message on my cell phone from Michelle, checking in on me and telling me all about her recent outings with her new friends over in Italy. It made me smile reading it; she was still in her own bubble, but I now admired her for it. I rolled my eyes and smiled, texting her back, saying that all was fine. Thinking over more personal life matters, and while I had my cell in my hands, I decided to check in on my personal email account to see whether anything interesting had gone on there.

As I flicked through the reams of spam emails, deleting them one by one, I did notice one email about leaving a review for an item that I'd purchased a while back. It was some bespoke balloons that I'd bought online for the twins birthday, and I had been pleased with my purchase at the time. I flicked onto the site, and it was saying how much I had paid, and when they had been delivered. As I looked at the price, I wasn't sure that I'd paid that much - I thought they were actually cheaper than that, so confused, I flicked onto my banking app to see whether I was mistaken.

Logging in, I had a look at my recent purchases, which mainly consisted of business transactions and the designer items that I'd splurged on, the day that Stephen had gotten on my nerves. I eventually found the purchase of the balloons, and I was mistaken about the price, so shrugged it off.

As I was about to log off, I remembered that on this app, I had the details of Stephen's account, which we had put in joint names. He was always open about his money, and had maintained that if I ever wanted the money back, then it was there. That was how I'd realized I could really trust him, and I had nothing to worry about with him where money was concerned. I had completely forgotten that his account was on here, so I swiped over to have a look, as it may have given me an idea of where he was.

As I swiped the page, his account details popped up on the screen, and I clicked on it to have a look at the transactions. A few was at a convenience store, and some shopping he had done, which was typical of him not to be splurging. As my eyes scanned over the relatively boring transactions, they suddenly widened as they reached a certain point on the statement - a point which made me sit further upright in my seat.

Further down the page, were three recent transactions, on three separate occasions, of fifty-thousand dollars, which had gone out of his account and had been debited goodness-knows-where. That was the only piece of information that did concern me because it was so unlike him to pay out for anything, let alone let that amount of money go. He had always been so reluctant to spend the money, because he was aware that it came from my father, and even though I'd practically pushed it on him, he only used it as and when he needed anything. He was pursuing his dream of being a physiotherapist, and often would use his wage to buy anything else.

Scrolling further down to see whether this was of a frequent occurrence, it seemed that this had only been happening recently when he was acting strangely. While a part of me thought that he had found somebody else and was splurging all this money on her, another part of me knew how rubbish that was. He was never free and easy with money like that, so either she was really worth doing it for, or something else was going on with him.

I sat, bolt upright, thinking over what he could've been doing with that money - images of him and another woman rolling around on a bed of money together and laughing at me, popping into my mind. I closed the app down and tossed my cell phone to one side. I wished I hadn't bothered looking now.

It was his money, and considering this was probably going to end up in divorce, he would get it anyway. I knew it was bullshit to be pulling a face over it. I had always told him to spend some extra money and be easier on himself, and then when he did, I'm in a mood! But the way he had been lately, should I really care? After what had happened with the baby, no, I probably shouldn't care one iota. I still felt hurt, though. It was the weirdest mix of emotion, and I couldn't go there in my own head.

Sitting in pure, deafening silence for a while, the ping of the doorbell shot through my thoughts. Snapping back to reality, I went to answer the door.

"Hi, Eleanor!" Tasha smiled.

"Oh, hi," I replied, still not really with it.

"Sorry, is this a bad time? I brought Darcy with me. I thought we could have a girly catch up!" she squealed.

My eyes shot to Darcy who was stood next to her, probably wondering what was wrong with me.

"No, no... sorry, girls. Come on in." I smiled, making way for them to enter through the doorway.

Tasha and Darcy stepped into the house and stood in the hallway while I closed the door behind them.

"Is everything okay, Eleanor?" Tasha eyed.

"Yeah, everything is fine. Come on through to the living area." I motioned for them to go and sit down.

Tasha and Darcy sat on the sofa and I went and sat on the recliner nearest to them.

"So anyway, me and Darcy have been talking, and we wondered whether you fancied coming with us to the local spa... make a girls day of it." Tasha grinned.

"Yeah, sorry about just dropping in, Eleanor," Darcy spoke. "It's just I thought it would be nice for us all to get together?" She smiled.

"Yeah, that sounds lovely. It is nice to see you again, Darcy," I replied back, not really feeling like I wanted a girls day, but maybe it was in order to cheer myself up.

Tasha sat forward in her chair. "Listen, Eleanor... we kind of know about Stephen. He said to my mom that he's left. Now, we're not interfering!" Tasha quickly exclaimed. "But you've always been a great sister-in-law to me, and it's just to let you know that me and my mom are not taking sides. We both love you... you've been there for both of us."

I softened at Tasha's statement. "Thanks, Tash. That's nice to know." I smiled her way and then remembered that Darcy was present in the room.

"Sorry, Eleanor. I'm kind of caught in the middle." Darcy chuckled. "I don't know what's going on really, but I like you, and I'd like us to be friends. So I'm also here if you ever need to talk. I've had relationships in the past that have turned sour, so I know how stupid men can be!" She laughed.

I laughed back. "Thanks, Darcy. That's really kind of you. And yeah, men are stupid." I grinned and then paused. "Yeah, you know what... a girl's day sounds like fun. I'm in. Let me grab my purse and we'll go."

"Yay!" Tasha cheered in her usual style.

"I'm driving and know where the place is, so you don't need anything else with you," Darcy stated.

"Great," I replied, grabbing my purse, as the three of us headed out of the door.

As we drove along to the spa, I sat in the backseat while Tasha rode shotgun next to Darcy. Darcy had a really nice car - it was a convertible Jaguar, and it was very plush. I was thinking to myself that I may invest in one for when I took the children places, as it was comfortable on the backseats. We chatted some more about what treatments were available at the spa, and I did chuckle to myself when I thought about how I had been forced into the idea of getting a massage. I desperately needed one, so this impromptu outing was probably ideal.

When we got to the spa, Darcy parked in the parking lot, and we made our way into what looked like an exclusive resort. I'd never actually been to this place before, so it was nice to go somewhere different. There were palm trees outside, and the sun drenched the white walls of the sterile, yet welcoming, looking building.

We stepped inside and were greeted at reception by a lady wearing a smock. Darcy whipped out her membership card, and it hadn't dawned on me that maybe you had to be a member here. Luckily money does talk, so after paying a bit extra, we booked what treatments we wanted and went inside.

The aromas of essential oils and the sound of soft music was intoxicating. It was blissful to be in such surroundings, and I was glad I'd taken them up on the idea of this outing. We all decided that we wanted to enjoy a nice massage together, so we undressed in a separate room and then wrapped fluffy white robes around ourselves. Next, we were shown into a room with massage tables, beautifully lit with candles, and what sounded like whale music playing in the background.

Lying on the table, I relaxed, as the massage therapist started to undo all the knots in my back. It felt utterly blissful to be receiving such attention. It had been so long since I'd had anything like this done, and I could have easily fallen asleep in the midst of it. I had a full body massage, and considering that this was supposed to be a girls day out, both Tasha and Darcy, who were on other tables, didn't utter a word. We were far to relaxed to talk.

Afterwards, we were served with some champagne and an offer of a swim, as we sat poolside in our robes with face masks on, feeling thoroughly contented.

"That was just what was needed," I remarked, leaning back on my lounger.

"Oh yes... I could seriously get used to living like this," Tasha agreed.

"The massages are excellent here," Darcy spoke. "I often come here after a stressful day at work."

"I need to do this more often. I've been promising myself a little pamper session for... well, years actually." I chuckled, sipping my champers.

"You need to look after yourself more, Eleanor. Shove what these men are like. They're the reason us ladies need facilities like these." Darcy chuckled.

"Too true." I laughed. "So what happened in your relationships, Darcy? If you don't mind me asking."

"No, not at all." She smiled. "Well, I've had a couple of long-term relationships, but I've never been married. I find that the men aren't suitable... so they have to go." She smirked.

"Why, what were they like?" Tasha wondered.

"Idiots. The lot of them. I had one serious boyfriend when I was younger, but he was way too clingy for my liking. I like my freedom, and he seemed to smother me," she explained.

"Yeah, men can be quite domineering... I get where you're coming from with that. It's easier being single, and when you want to do something, you don't have to ask permission." I grinned.

"Exactly. Men are only good for one thing, and sometimes they even fall short in that area." Darcy smirked.

I smirked back at her, as Tasha piped up. "So, Eleanor, what is happening with you and Stevie? Is it over for good?" she wondered, with her big hazel eyes peeping out from behind the face mask.

"I honestly don't know, Tash. I don't know what has gone on with him. Well, I have a fair idea. But the way he has been with me lately... I mean, I haven't heard from him in weeks! That's not the man that I married. I don't feel like I know him anymore."

"You're better off without," Darcy chipped in. "Sorry, Tasha. No offense to your brother."

"None taken. Me and my mom don't understand what's up with him," she pouted.

"Has he said where he's staying at the moment?" I wondered.

"No. He just said he needs time out. From previous experience, we know when he says that to leave him be. I wish I could help more, but I don't know anything else. Although I really don't want it to affect our friendship." Tasha smiled.

"I don't want it to, either. We've all been through a lot. You and your mom both mean the world to me. Plus we have children who are cousins, so it would be nice to keep relationships going for them," I soothed.

"Definitely." Tasha smiled, clinking her glass on mine.

"Here's to the future, ladies." Darcy smiled as she raised her glass. "May everything work out as planned, and the men folk rue the day." She grinned.

Me and Tasha laughed, leaning forward and clinking our glasses against hers, as we all took a big gulp of champagne in unison. This was one of the nicest afternoons I'd had in ages.

GETTING HOME THAT EVENING, after a having a spot of dinner with the ladies at a nearby restaurant, I stepped into the hallway and flung off my shoes. I felt so relaxed and carefree, and it had a wonderful day.

I'd agreed to meet up with Tasha and Darcy tomorrow, and said that they could come around to the house first, and we could have some lunch and then maybe do a bit of shopping. It was nice to have some ladies around me, as with Michelle away practically all of the time, I really didn't have as much female company as I would have liked.

I'd called through to the house and told Penny to go home earlier, which I think she was pleased about. Penny was close to her daughters, and one of them had recently had a baby, so she was taking to being a grandmother full throttle.

Natalie had taken the children up to bed, so I was glad of the peace and quiet. It was that kind of day, where as much R&R would be welcomed.

Wandering through to the kitchen, I decided that I wouldn't say no to another glass of champagne. I'd had one at the spa, and one over dinner, and thought that I may as well enjoy a third while I settled down on the sofa with my book and relaxed some more.

As I happily walked through to the living room clutching my flute of the good stuff, I took a sip of champagne before propping it on the coffee table, and sat back with my book. Just as I turned to the page I was up to, I was interrupted by the doorbell pinging.

Rolling my eyes, I heaved myself up from the sofa. It was typical to get a disruption when I wanted to relax. Making my way to the door, I opened it, and to my surprise it was Brandon.

"Hi, Eleanor." He smiled, waving a bottle of wine in the air. "Care for some company?"

"Er, yeah sure, come on in." I smiled, feeling surprised at seeing him on my doorstep, and moving out of the way to let him through.

Brandon moved through the doorway, into the hallway and then turned to face me. "I hope you don't mind the intrusion. I went to Rose Designs today, but I was informed you were taking a few days off. So I thought I'd come by and say hello... see if you wanted a little company?"

"I wasn't expecting anyone tonight, but it's lovely to see you. Come through to the kitchen and we'll open the wine. Although I was just about to enjoy a glass of champagne." I grinned.

Brandon followed me through to the kitchen, while I hunted down a glass for him.

"Oh, are you celebrating anything?" he wondered, placing the bottle of wine on the kitchen island.

"No, not really. Well, I suppose I am celebrating freedom." I chuckled.

"Freedom?" he echoed.

"Yeah, I think so. It's a long story," I answered, retrieving a glass for him. "Would you like some champagne instead? If you do, I'll put that bottle in the fridge."

"Yeah, champagne sounds good." He grinned, handing me the bottle of wine to put away, while I poured him a glass of crisp champers. "You can tell me all about it, if you like?"

"Come through to the living room and I'll fill you in."

We walked through to the living room and propped ourselves on the sofa together. Brandon was always a breath of fresh air, so it was nice to have him around. We sat and chatted, and I told him briefly about Stephen's change in moods, and how he had become distant with me. Then I told him about him leaving me, and how I had not heard from him since. I knew I hardly knew Brandon, but he had that air about him, that made me feel secure in the fact that I could tell him these things.

"Wow, sounds like you've been through the mill." He sighed, sipping his champers.

"Yeah. To be honest, though, I'd rather be alone than around someone like that. Plus if he's met someone else, and hasn't even got the balls to tell me, then I'm not going to play the victim. Me and my children deserve better than that. He's in contact with his mom and sister, so I know he's okay. It must be nice to switch off from your family like that," I huffed.

"So you think he's met someone else?" Brandon wondered.

"Yes. I'm almost a hundred percent certain on that one. It was the way he was with me... he wouldn't come near me. But I'm bordering along the lines of too much information here, so I won't give you the details!" I laughed.

"Don't worry," Brandon chuckled, "I think I get the picture. I've had my fair share of heartache in the past. I think it's something that we all go through at some point."

"Care to divulge what happened?" I asked, sipping my drink.

"Nothing really relevant... I've never been married. But I've been cheated on, and I know how much it hurts." Brandon leant back on the sofa as he reminisced and placed his arm along the back of where I was sitting. "I think that some people just stop valuing what they have with each other, you know?" He rested his eyes in mine, and I could see the hurt peeping through.

"Yeah, I do understand. I think that as relationships go along, you forget what initially you fought for. It becomes... comfortable... and it's just expected that the other person will always be there. Then when one of you changes, it can be devastating to the other party... if you get what I mean?" I smiled softly.

"I do know what you mean. My ex did change... they'd met someone else, but didn't care to inform me!" He laughed. "I don't agree with hurting someone that way. Do you?"

I looked into his eyes, and no, I didn't agree with hurting anyone like that. I'd always tried my best to be loyal to Stephen, yet having that stabbed in the back hurt like hell. Yet, here I was with Brandon, who seemed to be on the same wavelength, and it was so nice to be around him. I placed my hand on his chest and leant in nearer to him. I could feel a connection between us, and just as I was about to lean in to kiss him, he jumped bolt upright out of his seat.

"Sorry, Eleanor! I did not mean to give you the wrong impression!" he exclaimed, looking flustered.

"What? You mean... what?" I mumbled, wide-eyed and not knowing what to do with myself now sat on the sofa alone.

"You're a really lovely lady, but this is so not right," Brandon stated, looking horrified.

"Why? What's not right?" I asked, standing up. "You like me, don't you?"

"Yes, I do like you, but not in that way, sorry. Oh..." He sighed, putting his hands on his head and then reaching out to me and holding my hands. "I'm really sorry if I gave you the wrong impression. I do like you, but just as a friend."

I could feel the blush of embarrassment come over my face. This was so humiliating.

"Oh right," I mumbled, looking down at the floor.

"I like you, Eleanor. Can we please stay friends?" he half-begged.

"Er, yeah sure," I muttered, slowly raising my eyeline to finally look at him. "I'm sorry I did that."

"You don't have to be sorry. It was probably my fault. I maybe gave off the wrong vibe or something." He sighed, still holding my hands in his. "Anyway, I better go."

Brandon released my hands and made his way to the front door. I was going to show him out, but I seemed to be rooted to the spot. Hearing the door close behind him as he left, I finally moved and slumped down on the sofa by myself.

In that moment, I felt completely rejected. My husband had walked out on me, and the one man who had shown any interest, hadn't actually liked me that way at all. Was I really that ugly now? Maybe having three children and working my ass off had taken its toll on me, and I should resign myself to the fact that I wasn't attractive anymore.

Reaching over to my glass of champagne, I swilled the rest of it down in one big gulp. What had set out to be a drink of celebrating relaxation, had now turned into my consolation prize.

Chapter Six - Sleeping with the Enemy

It was a relief to have taken a few days off, because if Brandon would have turned up at work, I wouldn't have known where to put myself. In one respect, I couldn't believe I had practically thrown myself at him, and in another, I couldn't believe he had knocked me back. I wasn't sure whether I'd ever thrown myself at a man before, and being knocked back? Well, it didn't feel good.

I skulked about the house for the morning, until Tasha and Darcy came around for another girly afternoon. We upped sticks and took ourselves off to the mall, and it was good to take my mind off things. We shopped, chatted, and sipped cappuccinos, and it was all very girlish. Tasha was telling us how David was looking after Reece, and Darcy seemed thrilled that she had met her nephew and was now getting to know him.

I bought myself a few items, such as perfume and a new lipstick, but I didn't feel in the mood to splurge too much today. My confidence was shot, and I didn't feel like wasting my money on products that didn't seem to work anyway. Adverts that claimed I could have any man in the world in I used a certain face cream was a load of bull, and I wasn't in the mood to buy into the hype.

Tasha and Darcy could probably tell there was something amiss, but I certainly wasn't going to mention Brandon, and what had happened with him. I was embarrassed enough, without having to relive it in my mind. I tried my best to put the spring in my step, and successfully had a carefree afternoon.

Once we were done shopping, I offered for them to come back to the house where we could watch a movie and order pizza. Tasha and Darcy seemed happy enough with that plan, so we drove back to my house in Darcy's car, and were chattering away about what we had bought from the mall, when we stepped inside the hallway.

Hearing Penny in the kitchen pottering about, I went through to her first and told her we were having a takeaway, so she didn't need to make dinner. The past few days, she had been made quite redundant with me, but she was happy that she had been feeding the children and Natalie, so it didn't bother her too much. Penny was definitely like mother hen, and she wanted to make sure that she fed us up full of lovely food to make sure we were healthy and well.

Wandering back into the hallway where Tasha and Darcy were stood, I nodded at them to say that all was sorted, and then walked towards the living room. Opening the door, I stopped in my tracks when I saw who was sat on the sofa - Stephen.

He stood up and looked at me. "Eleanor, can we talk?" he asked.

Before I could say anything, Tasha and Darcy appeared behind me, looking in the room at him.

"Stevie!" Tasha beamed.

Stephen's face was a picture, as he stood there and went pale.

"Oh, hey, Tash. Listen, I'll just go." He walked through the living room, and we all moved out of the way to let him through the door.

Darcy and Tasha went into the living room, and I quickly closed the door over and caught up with Stephen, as he was about to exit through the front door.

"Wait," I called. "Why are you here? And where the hell have you been?" I angrily asked in a hushed tone.

He turned around to face me, just before he was about to leave. "I can't talk to you right now."

"That's not answering my question!" I snapped. "The children miss you."

A look of sadness crossed his eyes. "I know, I'm sorry. I can't..."

"I'm gathering you've met someone else," I cut in.

"No, well, yes. Well, not exactly."

My heart broke on the spot. My suspicions had been confirmed - he had been with another woman.

"Just go," I muttered, the tears brimming my eyes.

"Eleanor..." Stephen reached out to me.

Just before he could touch me, Darcy opened the living room door.

"Is everything all right, Eleanor?" she asked, sounding concerned.

Stephen turned away from me and bolted out of the door. I closed my eyes as I let the sensation of devastation wash over me. Stephen had broken my heart, and bashed all the pieces with that one sentence. Although deep inside I knew there was a strong possibility he'd met someone else, having it confirmed today, by both his words and body language, cut me into shreds.

Quickly wiping the brimming tears with my hand, I pulled myself together to turn to Darcy.

"Yeah..." I replied, forcing a smile.

"You don't look it," she soothed, as I walked toward her and she put her arm around my shoulders. "Sorry I interrupted that then."

"It's okay," I sniffed, desperately trying to hold back the tears. "It's probably best you did. My marriage is over."

TASHA WAS SAT IN STUNNED silence, which in turned surprised me: I'd never seen her so quiet. It seemed that even Tasha thought that we were one of the strongest couples she had ever known, and was surprised that something, or someone unknown, had been able to break us apart.

It kind of killed the mood for a movie and pizza, so they both said that they would leave me in peace and let me have some space. I was glad of that, as I didn't want to pretend to be all happy all night, like nothing was going on - I was heartbroken on the inside, and I wanted some time to come to terms with things.

When they left, I asked Penny whether she would make dinner for me, after all. She was surprised at my change of plans, but went with it as she could see that something was wrong. It was - my heart was missing a piece, and the rejection and hurt was overwhelming. All's I kept thinking was that Stephen would now be returning to this other woman, and sleeping in her bed. How disgusting.

I could hardly stomach any food when I thought about it, so I picked at my dinner and ate as much as I could without throwing up. Penny went home and told me to call her if I needed anything, and through pure chance, Clarisse called to ask if I was okay. I lied and told her everything was fine. I didn't want to talk about it at all.

Saying goodnight to the children before Natalie took them upstairs was heart-wrenching when I thought about whether they would see their daddy again. The doting daddy that adored his children, had now walked out on us to be with another woman, and it was all so sad. I shed a little tear after seeing Madison, as she was the double of Stephen, and she'd asked where he was. I couldn't explain to a five year old what was happening. I wasn't even sure I had the answer to that question myself.

Sitting myself on the sofa again, with a glass of wine and the bottle next to it, complete with a box of tissues, I flicked on the latest rom-com. I decided that I would be wallowing in my own self-pity for the night. It would serve to take my mind off my own love life - or lack of it - and I could cry as much as I wanted on my own, and not have to fight the tears anymore.

Before watching the movie, and out of curiosity, I decided to look at my banking app to see whether there were any transactions today from Stephen. Logging on, I clicked on his bank statement and noticed that another fifty-thousand dollars had been transferred again - this afternoon.

My blood boiled, yet ached, at the thought that he was no doubt splurging on treating the other woman to drown out the thought of me from today. Goodness knows what he was doing with that money - probably hiring private jets and heading off on luxurious vacations. I was torturing myself looking at this app, so I logged off and decided I wouldn't be doing that again.

Flinging my cell phone to the side of me, I flicked on the movie, as I sat back with my glass of wine and a tissue in hand - I was ready for any upcoming emotional outbursts. As I watched on, the movie went through the usual motions of boy meets girl, they fall in love, something keeps them apart, and then they end up back together. As lame and predictable as it was, I found tears streaming down my face as the credits rolled.

The music played as the movie finished, when suddenly the doorbell rang and interrupted my whinge-fest. Widening my eyes and wiping my cheeks down with the tissue, I rose from the sofa to go and answer the door.

"David!" I half-shouted, shocked by the sight of him stood at the other side of the threshold.

"Hello, El." He smirked. "Am I interrupting?" He chuckled at the sight of my bloodshot eyes.

"What? Oh, er, no... sorry, I was just watching a movie," I replied, wiping my face down some more. "Come in."

Moving out of the way to let the most unexpected person walk through the front door, why was he here? Should I be letting him in?

Wow, if Stephen was here right now, he probably would've frogmarched David down the steps. But he wasn't here, and under the upset surface, I was angry about that fact.

David turned to face me. "Sorry to intrude on your time."

I sighed. "Listen, I'm not sure why you're here, but if you've come to cause trouble... well, Stephen isn't here, and I'm too worn out to be bothered."

"I know he's not here. That's why I came to see you," he replied.

"Oh, so you knew I'd be on my own... perfect time to cause trouble then, David!" I snapped.

"No, you've got me all wrong," he protested, while I raised an eyebrow at that statement. "I only came to see if you were okay. Tasha told me about him leaving. To be honest, I was pretty shocked."

Ah yes, Tasha could never hold her own water where David was concerned.

"So you've come to gloat?" I genuinely wondered.

"No," he chuckled. "Listen, I'm not gonna lie, I was never his number one fan, but I was surprised when I heard about him walking out on you. If anything, I think he's an idiot."

Looking at David, I wondered whether this was some sort of game, but honestly, I couldn't have given a damn if he was up to anything.

"Come through to the living room. I don't want to disturb the children."

He walked with me and we went and sat down on the sofa together. I offered him a glass of wine, and when he accepted I got myself along to the kitchen to get him one. As I reached for the glass and took it back with me to the living area, I thought how extraordinarily weird this scenario was. My husband had left me, and now my ex-husband was going to be sharing a glass of wine with me.

No time machine necessary - I wouldn't even begin to know how to explain this to my past self.

Filling up our glasses, I handed him his as he thanked me. It seemed the more normal David was present with me tonight.

"How's your job going?" I asked, breaking the silence.

"Fine, yeah. I'm generally getting on with my life now and trying to make amends. I'm just trying to do the best by Reece."

"Fair enough. You seem to be doing your best. We have noticed," I replied.

"We?" he echoed.

"Well, me, mainly. You know Stephen doesn't exactly regard you as one of his buddies." I smirked.

"Hmm, that has been made apparent to me on more than one occasion." He winked, as he sipped his drink.

"How are things with Tasha? I gather you two are trying to make a go of things?" I asked, getting some truth out of him while I had the chance to.

"Things with Tasha are fine. Although we're not together, or anything like that. I think it's a wise decision not to be."

I sat back in amazement. "How so?" I wondered.

"When I was in rehab, I had a lot of therapy. I eventually saw my relationship with Tasha as being based on destruction. I cared for her, but while I was still harboring feelings for somebody else, it wasn't fair to string her along. I think she sees that now, but she's fine with it. She seems quite happy in her own little world... as long as I pay for it." He grinned.

"Yes, I had noticed that Tasha does like to be a lady of leisure. But if you're not together, then aren't you just supposed to be paying for Reece?" I asked.

"Supposedly. But to be honest with you, I don't mind. I put her through a lot at such a young age. I kind of feel like I am paying off my debt by looking after her too."

"Wow, you surprise me." I chuckled. "The new and improved David, eh?"

"You could say that. Although some things never change..."

"Like...?"

"Like you, my feelings," he replied, looking down at the glass in his hands.

Watching him for a moment, I actually did feel sorry for him. I had known him longer than I had known Stephen, and the transformation was pretty mind-blowing. The cockiness wasn't there anymore, and I wondered how different things would have been if I would have met him now, when he was like this, rather than all those years ago.

"Oh, I've changed." I chuckled, trying to break the silence that was looming over us. "I'm more hard-headed than I was years ago... age kind of toughens you up."

David lifted his line of sight to me. "You are still beautiful though, El... that will never change. You have an air about you like no other. The way you move, the way you talk... the way you care about everybody. The way you get a twinkle in your eye when you are laughing at something... it's the small things which make you stunning. I've never gotten over that. I don't think I ever will."

Wow - I was floored. From all the rejection that I had faced lately, that was the most wonderful thing I could hear. I placed my glass on the coffee table, and in a moment of madness I reached over and cupped David's face in my hands. This time, there was no rejection, as he also placed his glass down and moved closer toward me. I could see the longing in his eyes - the look that I had desperately needed to see, as he smoothly brushed his hands around my waist and steadily placed his lips onto mine.

We kissed with such ease, and it took me back to a time when my life was a lot simpler than it was now. It was nice to feel wanted, to feel loved, and as he tugged at my clothes and I removed his shirt to reveal that lovely ripple of muscle underneath, I longed to be touched and to feel at one with someone again.

Straddling him, he sat there on the sofa, wanting more of me and enjoying every moment of it, and I didn't mind providing him with what he wanted. Hands all over my body as we kissed and moved together in sequence, I blocked the whole world and it's mess out for a short while.

As we both reached an explosive end, I sagged into his arms from the exhaustion of losing myself. Snapping back, I pushed myself up, removing my legs from around him, and started to look around for my clothes. I didn't want to stay in his arms, or relish in the moment - what was done, was done, and I wasn't sure how I felt about it now that it was over.

"Wow, El." David smiled, as he fastened his jeans and started to place his shirt back on. "I never thought that would happen between us ever again."

"Yeah, er... neither did I." I disinterestedly muttered, as I looked half-naked around the living room for where I had flung my bra.

"I don't know what you want to happen now...?" he continued.

"Happen?" I asked, standing upright and holding my bra in my hands before starting to place it on.

"Yeah, happen between you and me... us." He grinned.

"David, nothing is going to happen with us. It was a one off, okay?" I half-snapped, as I put my t-shirt back on.

"But, El, after that, I thought you might want to..."

"Might want to what?" I asked, hand on hip and wondering what he was going on about. "Listen, it was a spur of the moment thing... it didn't mean anything. I don't even know whether it should have happened now or not."

"You can't tell me that that wasn't fantastic, El. We definitely click. We always have done," he continued.

I sighed heavily. "Ah, just stop!" I snapped. "That was great, yeah, but my marriage has just broken up, and I suppose I was looking for a bit of fun for a moment. I'm still in love with Stephen. I can't help it. I'm sorry, David."

David's face dropped as I spoke those words. A part of me felt guilty that I'd just subjected David to the one thing that I was hurting myself over - rejection. David grabbed his car keys that he had next to him, and made his way out of the house, closing the door behind him.

Sitting back down, I placed my head in my hands. What was already a mess, was now a total disaster.

WAKING UP IN THE MORNING, I couldn't believe that I'd had sex with David the night before. What the hell was I thinking? I was obviously handling this breakup with Stephen really well - and being optimistically sarcastic along the way.

I hauled myself out of bed. My few days off had ended, and it was back to work today.

As I got into the shower to wash away the whole scenario, and memory, of straddling my ex-husband on the sofa, I thought about what Stephen would make of this. He would disown me anyway now, but I suppose he had already done that.

Wow, my days off work had been a real success - and yes, I was still being sarcastic!

After showering, I noticed my wedding ring and the beautiful eternity ring that Stephen had bought me, lying on my bedside table. The little pearl in the centre was now representing the tears that I had shed. I sighed as I held it for a moment. A sign of his eternal love for me? What a crock of crap that was. Placing it in my bedside draw out of sight, I dressed in my suit and headed downstairs - I wanted to locate Roger.

With Penny calling 'good morning' out to me, as I waved and greeted her back, I entered the salon to find Roger dutifully waiting for me with a brush in his hand.

"Chica! Good morning!" he beamed my way.

"Hey, Roger, how are you today?" I smiled, sitting myself in his magic chair.

"I'm good, thanks. How are you?" He eyed me, narrowing his eyes as if he suspected something.

"I'm fine, yeah..." I warily replied. I paused as he stood there looking at me in the reflection of the mirror. "What's up, Roger?" I asked, my gaze still fixed on him.

"Oh nothing, nothing..." He grinned.

"Spit it out, Roger... the riddles are annoying." I grinned back.

"Well..." He crept to the side of me, and knelt down next to my chair, "I was here this morning when Penny was cleaning up. We found, erm... a little something in the living room."

Oh geez - what had they found?

"Like what?" I hesitantly wondered.

Roger nervously cleared his throat. "A condom packet.'" He smirked.

Oh my word - if the ground could've opened up now, that would've been fantastic. Even if I'd wanted to lie, my face gave the game away, as the heat of embarrassment flushed through my cheeks. Last night, I had been that mortified, that I'd forgotten all about the 'protection' we had used. I sighed and leant my head in my hand.

"How embarrassing," I whispered, wishing to be anywhere but here. "What must Penny be thinking."

"Hey, Chica, we are all grownups!" Roger chuckled. "So tell me, when did Stephen get back then, eh? A little nooky-nooky last night..." He winked.

Now this was even worse.

"It wasn't Stephen," I mumbled, not even being able to look him in the eyes.

"Eh?" Roger gasped, standing up. "Well, if it wasn't Stephen, who was it?"

I finally removed my head from my hand and looked up at him.

"You really want to know?" I asked, as Roger nodded like an excited puppy. "It was David."

"David?!" Roger exclaimed.

"Shh! Roger, please!" I waved my hands at him to try and shut him up. "I don't want the whole house knowing!"

He lowered his voice and leant into me. "But, David?! *The* David?!" he gasped again.

"Yes, but it was a one off and a mistake. Please don't say anything. Undoubtedly this will come out at some point, but I'm cringing thinking about what happened. It was really stupid. I don't know what anyone will make of this when they find out." I sighed.

"Oh, Chica... you must have been desperate," Roger soothed as he patted my shoulder.

"Thanks!" I laughed, feeling shocked and amused at the statement.

Roger laughed. "No, I didn't mean it that way! It's just, David? I can't believe it! I never thought that would happen ever again! You hated him so much!"

"I know. I also remember how much he hurt me as well. I'm so confused. He came round last night to see if I was okay, because he'd heard from Tasha that Stephen had left. One thing led to another, and well, you know the rest..."

"Ah yes, the want of somebody to feel close to you again."

"Exactly!" I hastily agreed. "But then David started talking about 'us', and I snapped at him, and he left... oh my word, it's one big mess!" I breathed out heavily.

"Don't worry. We all make mistakes. But what are you going to do?" he wondered.

"Nothing. Well, not nothing. I'm going to carry on with my life, and see how things work out. I suppose one of the first things that I will have to deal with, is divorcing Stephen."

"Really?!" Roger gasped.

"Well, yeah... he's moved on. We can't stay married forever. Plus he's hurt me, and no matter how much I still love him, I can't forget that. It would be unrealistic for us to stay married now that we have both been tainted by infidelity. One day he'll no doubt want to marry someone else... as will I. I will sit back in my old age and laugh about all of this, surrounded by ten cats and wondering how I had the time to be married eight times, and divorced." I chuckled.

Roger laughed. "You okay, though? You seem okay when you are talking about it."

"I'm hurting, Roger. But, I will come through this." I smiled softly.

"Good girl." He patted my shoulder and stood behind me again, as he started on my hair and makeup for the day.

After a while, Rogers creation was finished, and I looked and felt better being more glammed up. I went through to the kitchen to collect some breakfast from Penny, and I cringed when I thought about what she had found. Bless her, she didn't say anything, and just wished me a good day as I headed out of the door.

Driving along to Rose Designs, I felt a little more carefree. I loved driving, and was one thing that did make me feel happy - the freedom of being able to go out and dawdle along the winding roads for a while. There was nobody to bother me there, and I liked that - it seemed I was safer when kept away from other people.

Getting into work, Clarisse called out to me, and mouthed at me whether I was okay. I smiled and nodded, and continued my journey to my office. As I settled in my chair and started the working day, there was a knock at the door.

"Come in!" I shouted to whoever it was.

As I looked up, Jeanie popped her head around the door.

"Hi, Eleanor. Is it okay if I come in?" she asked politely.

"Of course, Jeanie, come on in." I smiled, stopping what I was doing, and waved at her to take a seat. "How can I help you?"

Jeanie sat down and gently smiled. "I just wanted to say I'm so sorry about what has happened between you and Stephen." She sighed. "I can't make head nor tail of it."

"Me neither, Jeanie," I agreed. "But I can't make him stay with me if he doesn't want to."

"I know what you mean. I wanted to see you to say that I love you like my own daughter, Eleanor, and I don't want to be in the middle of this. I would still like it if we could maintain a close relationship," she soothed.

"Of course." Standing from my seat, I went around my desk and propped myself on the edge of it to be nearer to her. "I don't want you to be unhappy because of this. Stephen has made his decision, and we all need to move on.

I would really like it if things ticked along as normal with us. I don't think Stephen would mind that, either."

"No, he wouldn't. I've told him that I won't reject you because of his behavior. To be honest with you, I'm really shocked at him. Leaving you is something that I would have never thought he would do in a million years."

"Tasha pretty much said the same the last time I saw her. I honestly haven't got the answer as to why this has happened. I guess he just met someone else and decided he didn't want me anymore." I sighed.

"That's the thing, though," Jeanie began, sitting further forward on her chair, "I don't think he is with anyone else."

"What do you mean?" I asked, with confusion seeping over me.

"This is what I'm unsure of. He has done something wrong, I know it, but I don't think he is with anyone else. I don't get that impression at all."

"Where is he? Has he said where he's staying?"

"No. He said he's with a friend." She sighed, sitting back.

"There you go, Jeanie. He is with someone else. He's using the 'friend' word to cover it up."

"No, this is different. If he was, he would tell me. I know that as well. He knows I'm not stupid, and I will get the truth out of him. He has always maintained that he is nothing like his father. That pig couldn't keep his thing in his pants for longer than an hour," Jeanie fumed, thinking back.

"That's true. When we saw his father, Matthew, all those years ago, Stephen was so angry at him and his cheating ways. But people change, things change. Maybe he realized that he didn't love me as much as he thought he did."

"He definitely loves you. I can hear it in his voice when he mentions your name."

"He talks about me?"

"Yes, all the time. He asks whether I've seen you, and if I know how you're doing. He also told me that you are expecting another baby." Jeanie smiled.

I closed my eyes at those words - I had to tell her.

"Jeanie, I was expecting, but I lost the baby," I replied sadly.

"Oh no!" she gasped, holding her hands up to her mouth.

She stood up and brought me into a hug. I closed my eyes and let the warmth radiate from her - she was a huge comfort to me. After a moment she pulled away.

"When did this happen?" she softly whispered.

"A couple of weeks ago. I went through it alone, and I'm so angry at Stephen for not being there. So you see, there's other things here, that no matter what, I'm finding very hard to forgive."

She sat back down and rested her hand on mine. "Of course you are... that is totally understandable. You should have told me. I would have been there for you."

"I know you would have. But I'm dealing with it, and trying to move on. I'm fine," I reassured.

"Do you want me to let Stephen know?"

"Yes, please. I think he has a right to know." I sighed.

"I'll let him know when he next calls. I'm not sure when that will be."

"Whenever is fine. I'm not expecting to talk to him anytime soon. He did appear at the house a few days ago, though."

"Did he? He never said anything about that," Jeanie replied, looking surprised.

"Yes, he appeared at the house and said he wanted to talk to me, but I had Tasha and Darcy with me. Have you met Darcy?"

"No. I've heard her name through Tasha. She's David's sister, right?"

"Yes. She's lovely, and we'd all been out doing a bit of shopping. So when we arrived back, they were with me, and Stephen obviously didn't want to talk in front of them, so he left. I haven't heard anything since."

"He didn't say he'd seen you. That is surprising."

"How so?"

"Because when I last spoke to him, he said that he had to keep his distance. I don't know what he's doing."

"You and me both. But I suppose time will tell. If you could tell him the unfortunate news about the baby, I would be grateful." I sighed.

"Of course. Anyway," Jeanie stood up from her seat, "I'll let you get on with your work. And please, if you ever need me, or need to talk, come and see me. My door is open for you day or night. I would like to visit the grandchildren soon, if that's okay? I really miss them." She smiled.

"Of course it is." I smiled back. "You are welcome anytime. And thanks for the chat."

Jeanie shot me a little nod and smile, before making her way out of my office and closing the door behind her. She was one of the strongest, yet sweetest ladies that I'd ever had the pleasure of knowing. There was no way I wanted what was happening with Stephen, to ruin the relationship I had with her.

I sat, still perched on my desk, as I mulled over what Jeanie had told me. She didn't think that he was seeing someone else, but she knew he had done something wrong. Did that excuse his behavior? Not in my book. Then again, with all that had happened, I didn't know what to think anymore.

As I lost myself in my usual thought bubble, my cell rang and broke through my current gravy train of thoughts.

"Hello?" I answered.

"Eleanor! Just to let you know that everything is ship-shape and underway," Mr. Franks called out on the other end.

"Ah, brilliant, thank you so much," I replied, smiling to myself.

"I think Caroline will be coming to see you this morning. You need to sign a few things, and it would be good for you both to discuss in person what is expected from either party. It's all legally done and dusted, but it's wise to get together with your investor as and when, to go over these things."

"That's great. I can't thank you enough for your help – again." I chuckled.

"You're very welcome. Although I will admit that it has been rather lucrative working with Caroline, so it's been a pleasure." He laughed.

"I'm glad." I laughed back.

"So, how is everything with yourself?" he asked.

"Good, yes. Well, sort of okay. I may require your help again soon." I sighed.

"How so?" he asked, with his animated tone coming down a notch.

"I think I'll be getting a divorce."

"Oh," came the sullen reply.

"Things haven't worked out how I hoped with Stephen... well, Mr. Rose is how you know him."

"If you don't mind me asking, Eleanor, why?"

"He's left me, and I think he's met someone else. I don't want to divorce on the grounds of adultery, though... it'll be through irreconcilable differences. He changed, and I'm not putting up with it anymore."

"I must say that it is very sad news. I never thought I would have been having to draw up divorce papers for that marriage. That is quite shocking," Mr. Franks replied.

"I know. I don't think anyone saw it coming, but I suppose never say never."

"No indeed. Life has a funny way of throwing you the least likely of events."

"You can say that again." I chuckled. "You have been there through most of mine."

"Indeed." I could hear him grin on the other end of the line. "Well, whenever you need me, pick up the phone and I'm there. I must go now, because I have a client waiting."

"No problem. Thanks again, and I will speak to you soon."

The phone went down and the conversation was over. It did make me smile when I thought about how friendly I was with Mr. Franks. Nowadays, he even called me Eleanor, which I didn't mind at all. Was anyone else ever this friendly with their lawyer? I'd needed him that much over the years, that it was no wonder he was on a first name basis with me. Out of respect of him being an elder, I wouldn't have dreamt of calling him by his first name. He knew my father and had stuck by him - he was due total respect when and where I could give it to him.

Sat at my desk again, there was another knock on the door. It seemed that I was the most popular woman on the planet today. I shouted for them to come in, and this time Caroline walked in with her bodyguards waiting outside.

"Caroline, hi!" I greeted as she walked through.

"Hi, Eleanor. I hope you don't mind me dropping by." She smiled, as she closed the door and came and took a seat.

"No, not at all. I've just spoken to Mr. Franks, who said that you would be coming over this morning." I chuckled. "Your ears must have been burning."

"Ah, at least you were forewarned." She chuckled back.

Caroline's stern front had definitely eased up since I had gotten to know her better.

"So, I hear everything is done and dusted on the legal front, which is excellent news." I smiled.

"Yes, and I have some papers here that are for you to sign. Take your time and read through them all. I asked Mr. Franks for them because I wanted to see you personally today." Caroline pulled out the papers from under her coat and slid them over the desk to me.

"Thank you," I replied, taking hold of them. "I'll have a read over them later. I'm sure everything is above board. So how come you wanted to see me today?"

"I came by to see if you would accompany me to the new premises. I would like to see around them and how everything is coming along, and see if I can start pitching a few ideas your way."

"That sounds great," I beamed. "Any help is greatly appreciated. I've got to say, I'm excited to be working with you. You took me by surprise when you first said you wanted to become an investor. You have a wealth of knowledge which is invaluable."

"I appreciate the sentiment, Eleanor." She smiled warmly at me.

"I've got to ask, though, how come you chose Rose Designs? Surely you could invest in any business you liked."

"I know a good opportunity when I see one. Plus, I like you... I think with a little nurturing you could be one of the finest businesswomen around. You don't give up, and I like that. I know that my money is well placed."

"That is quite a compliment." I grinned. "Anyway, would you like to go and look at the new premises now? They are due to open soon."

"Yes, let's. My driver will take us there."

Grabbing my purse, I followed Caroline out of the door to where her security were waiting to escort us to her car. This was all very different for me, as I was used to going about my business and not having to think about anyone following me around, and it made me ponder upon how Caroline's life was so different. I did wonder whether the prospect of even more money in the bank would finally deduce me to living like that, yet I wasn't sure I was entirely comfortable with that notion. I liked my freedom, and that did not include having security waiting on the other side of the door of the bathroom.

Using Caroline's flashy chauffeur-driven car, we reached the new premises which was in the heart of the city. Eventually, I was going to hire a manager who would look after the place, and I would take a step back and dot in and out when I wanted to.

Opening up the doors with my set of keys, I let Caroline, and her bodyguards, into the building. All that was really left was the decorating, which of course my designers were onto at the moment.

Standing in the empty foyer, with bare walls and an echo which only seemed to come with a building that was not yet in use, Caroline started to look around.

"What do you think?" I asked, as she eyed the ceilings and walls.

"Very good. I think this is a marvellous place," she replied, then turned to face me. "Do you want my business opinion, though?"

"Of course. With you being an investor, pitch in wherever you feel like," I stated.

"I think you should have a store on the ground floor," she answered in all seriousness.

"A store? But online shopping is far outdoing any high street retail," I replied.

"Not everybody shops online, Eleanor. You are missing a whole line of custom right there."

"So what do you propose, then?" I wondered.

"I propose that you convert this whole floor space as a store, to display your bespoke designs. Perhaps slightly lower your retail price, as there are people with not as much money who would like your items. It's not just about the rich... you have to include all audiences."

"So just a store to sell items in, for everybody?"

"Yes. Make cups, cutlery, canvases... household items that appeal to every person who walks past here. Like a designer boutique, but more affordable. Not everyone can splash the cash. Then you have your premises just above here where you carry out work, and any clients can go up for a designated appointment. I think it would broaden your market and increase your income."

"You do have a point, Caroline. Putting it that way, I actually think a store could be a really good idea. I've been so fixated on the website, and bringing in multi-million pound contracts, that I've overlooked that part."

"That's why you bring in investors." Caroline smiled. "Between the both of us, we could smash this market."

"I'm going to have to start looking for store assistants... and a manager," I thought out loud.

"No need. I have staff that would be very well suited."

"You do?" I wondered.

"I have a wealth of contacts, Eleanor."

"True. So you could handle that for me?"

"Of course. I have the perfect person who could be your manager as well." She grinned.

"Who?" I wondered - that was quick.

"David." She smiled.

I shook my head in confusion. "David? Like *the* David... the David who was your nephew, and who you once termed as being a scoundrel, David?"

"Yes." Caroline broadly smiled.

"Seriously? Is this a joke?" I wondered - wondering whether I would wake up at any moment and this would have all been some kooky dream.

"Yes, I'm serious. It's true that I didn't particularly think much of him in the past, but when my late-husband passed, I got to find out a few home truths about him. I realized how he was basically groomed by that horrible man, and a lot of damage had been done. I monitored his progression while he was in re-hab, and I've been keeping tabs on him since. He reached out to me not long ago to make amends... he's definitely a far cry from the man we once knew."

"But, Caroline, the man tried to fleece me of Pearl Designs... and in the end he actually won! I can't take him on here!" I protested, thinking about last night as well, but there was no way I was telling Caroline that part.

"Think about it, Eleanor... I know what he's been like in the past, but I didn't know the true extent of it until it all blew up that night at the hotel. I'm not taking my eye off the ball with him ever again... you have my word on that." Caroline came and stood in front of me. "He could charm the birds from the trees, he has the gift of the gab, and the looks to match. Utilized in the right di-rection, he could make this place a success in no time."

Mulling it over for a moment, Caroline had her determined gaze fixed right on me. She was right - David was very good at persuading people to do pretty much anything. Let's face it, I'd hand first-hand experience of that. Plus he did seem to be drastically turning his life around, and if I gave him the managerial position, it would ease my own conscience after rejecting him last night straight after our little 'encounter'.

"Fine. So are you going to approach him with the offer?" I wondered.

"No, I thought you could do it. Ultimately, you are in charge of the hiring and firing, Eleanor. I actually want to be more backseat on this. If he thinks this has come from me, then he'll think I'm some sort of soft touch. I am by no means a soft touch, so it's better if you deal with it. The less he knows about me being involved, the better."

"Okay," I sighed. "I'll speak to him."

"Brilliant!" Caroline smiled. "Come then, let's have a look at the rest of the building."

We wandered around the rest of the premises, while I informed Caroline of my plans for the place. She seemed happy with what I had in mind, and chirped in every now and then with a few ideas. She did seem to want to have a big say in how things were done, and that I didn't really mind. She had fantastic business acumen, and if any of the workload was taken from me, then that was even better.

When myself and Caroline parted ways and I was dropped back off at the Rose Designs headquarters, I could feel both the ache in my mind and feet. I was drained with all that was going on, and with what was also happening at home. I was in need of another break, but I soldiered on and carried out my working day as per usual, until it was time to go home. I seemed to be bombarded with things that other people needed at the moment, and I couldn't take any more on board.

As soon I got home, I slipped off my shoes and headed in to see Penny, to get something to eat.

"Hello, Miss. Eleanor!" Penny greeted as I walked through. "My, you look tired."

"I am, Penny. I think I need a vacation." I sighed, sitting down at the breakfast table.

"Can you take a vacation?" she wondered, handing me a cup of tea.

"Not right now. I've got the expansion, and investors, and hiring more staff... plus the contracts are still pouring in. Also there's the children to consider, and with Stephen not around anymore, and argh! I can't think straight." I sighed, folding my arms on the table and resting my head in them.

"You know, Miss. Eleanor, you are thinking too much about all of this. You need to break it down... relax..." Penny chuckled.

"How?" I muffled through my arms.

"By doing one thing at a time. Stop applying all the pressure to yourself. One job at a time, and it soon becomes a smaller and smaller task."

"You're right," I agreed, sitting back up. "And I know what I have to tackle first. What time do you finish, Penny?"

"In about half an hour. Why?" she wondered.

"No reason. It's just I don't mean to sound awful, but there's something I have to do alone tonight."

With all due respect to Penny, I wanted to see David, and I didn't want her to be around. She was right that I had to take things one step at a time, and that was the first thing on the agenda. If anything, I suppose it was a matter of keeping my enemies close, and this time I would not be made a fool of by any man. I'd had enough of that to last a lifetime.

After eating dinner and wishing Penny a goodnight, I hastily made my way to my cell to text David. I knew that as soon as I text him, he would be around here like a shot. I surprised myself at my dealings with him lately, but hey, never say never. My life was always unpredictable.

Chapter Seven - Interference

I text David and waited - I heard nothing. As I was about to give up on the idea of him getting back to me, the doorbell rang. Lo and behold, there he was, stood at the other side of the door - I knew he couldn't keep away.

"Hi, David," I politely greeted. "Come on in."

Moving out of the way, he stepped through. Ushering him into the living room, he sat down on the sofa, and I swear we both gave a little sideways glance to the part of the sofa that we'd got a bit 'hot and heavy' on last night.

"You wanted to see me?" he replied, very matter-of-factly.

"Yes, I did. Thanks for coming."

David sighed. "Listen, El, I know that in the past I've been..."

"Shh," I interrupted. "I've not called you here to talk about anything like that."

David turned to face me and arched an eyebrow. "What did you want to talk to me about, then?"

"I have a proposition for you," I coolly stated, sitting back and placing my business head firmly on.

"Proposition?" David paused for a second, looking off into the distance, and then turned back to me. "Oh right, I see what this is." He grinned.

"Which is...?" I asked, feeling perplexed.

"This." He smiled, moving his hands backwards and forwards between both of us.

"You've lost me," I replied, still not getting what he was actually talking about. Had he already spoken to Caroline?

David chuckled. "You want to set up a little agreement between the both of us. Like a booty call, and to keep it to myself. I'm fine with that if it means I can be with you in some way. I agree that it's not a good idea to tell Tasha, and even though you two are over, you won't want to tell driver, er, I mean, Stephen about this."

"Whoa! Hold up!" I exclaimed, standing up. "That's not why I called you here."

David stood up to face me. "Really?" he half-squealed in his manly tone. "Why did you want to see me? Last night you seemed pretty adamant that you wanted me out of here, after we... you know..." David turned his eyeline toward the sofa.

Finding myself grinning slightly at the thought, David caught me smiling. I cleared my throat and pulled myself together - I wasn't some teenager now.

"No, that's not what my reason for calling you here tonight was!" I protested.

"Oh, come on, El..." He grinned, edging closer toward me, and sliding his hands around my waist. "You know it was good. I've never had sex like it. It leaves me wanting more."

I softened in his arms for a moment, feeling the rush of heat fill me as he pressed his body against mine. But no, this was not why he was here - and this was *still* David!

I pulled away. "Stop. That's not why I wanted to speak with you. Can we just sit normally for a moment, like two rational adults?"

Taking a seat on the sofa, I willed the heat that was rushing through my body to go away. I couldn't believe that I was back here with him, and actually feeling these things.

"Fine." David grinned, as he sat back down as if butter wouldn't melt. "What was it you wanted to ask me?"

"I wanted to ask you something about Rose Designs," I began.

"You wanted to ask me something about your business?" he asked, looking both baffled and amused at the statement.

"Yes. The reason I called you here tonight, was because I'm opening a store in town, and I was wondering whether you wanted the managerial position?"

David burst out laughing. "You want me to work for you?!" he roared with laughter.

"Yes, why is that so funny?" I grinned.

David settled himself and moved closer to me, taking my hand in his. "El, you never cease to amaze me." He smiled. "You do realize that you are talking to the guy whom you used to be married to, who then betrayed your trust, and then worked in cahoots with a deranged psychopath to take your business away from you?"

When he put it like that, I seriously doubted Caroline's judgement on this one.

"Well, yeah... as insane as that now sounds." I sniggered. "That deranged psychopath is out of the picture, though, and you've come a long way since those days. I've seen you in action at work. You have the gift of the gab which works a charm on clients... and let's face it, I've fallen for it myself on one or two occasions." I chuckled. "I think if correctly utilized, you could do wonders for a business. It would beat your salary at Jefferson's, and that in turn provides more for Reece. It's family first with me every step of the way, David. You should know that by now."

"Hmm..." he murmured as he sat back. "That I do know about you. When would the position start?"

"I'd say in a few weeks' time. Enough time for you to work your notice, and then you jump straight in with us. You know the ropes of designing and selling, and I'd trust you to do it proud."

"Eleanor Pearl, or should I say Rose,' He smirked, "I never thought I would ever be here with you like this again, never mind working for you." David paused for a moment, as he looked on at me in an intrigued way. "Yeah, I'm in. You are now looking at your new store manager. It is an offer I simply cannot refuse," he joked, grinning at me.

"Two offers in two days. My, you are doing well." I grinned back. "Shall we toast to new working relationships?"

"Why not."

He smiled that pearly smile, as I got up and went to get two glasses and a bottle of champagne. It did seem to be a staple piece in this house, and I was partial to a glass or two every now and then - or every night, given half a chance.

I strode back into the living room with the bottle and two glasses, filling them up and then handing one to David.

"To us!" David toasted as he raised his glass toward mine as I sat back down.

"To working relationships," I corrected and grinned, and clinked my glass against his.

David took a gulp of champagne before talking. "So you not heard anything from Stephen, then?" he asked.

"Nope," I replied, swallowing my champagne and feeling it go down like a brick at being asked that question.

"He is a stupid man, El," David remarked, looking over at me.

"I'm inclined to agree. But I haven't had the best track record when it comes to my marriages." I smirked.

"Touché." He smiled. "I think love makes all men stupid. We can't think straight. Or maybe that is just being around you." He sniggered, taking a sip of more champagne.

"Whatever it is, I wish you men would stop it. I've had enough of being messed around." I sighed.

David's face turned serious. "Don't jump down my throat for saying this, but you do know that if you ever changed your mind about being with me, I would make it my business to never mess you around again. I hate myself for what I did in the past... there's so much I would love to erase. If I could go back now, I would tell that deranged uncle of mine to shove it, and just be there for you. I am truly sorry for everything that went on. I was naive, foolish, and had a cocaine habit that seemed to have me in its grips. I was a mess."

"I believe you," I stated, shocking myself with the words in the process. "I think we were all fairly naive, though. If I could go back, I would do things so differently."

"Like steer clear of me, no doubt." He chuckled.

"Yes, that would be the plan." I laughed.

David winked at me, taking another sip of champagne and looking relaxed. "I'm glad you didn't, though."

"Didn't what?"

"Steer clear of me," he replied.

"I don't think I could agree as much." I grinned. "But why do you say that?"

"Because you taught me what love really is. I had no idea before then. Yes, in my own strange way I thought I knew what it was... but no, love is kind and caring... you were always those things. Plus you had a smoking rack on you, which always helps!" David laughed.

"David!" I yelled in embarrassment.

He continued to laugh. "What? It's true! Having a private viewing last night brought it all back to me!" He roared with laughter.

"Oh my word... shut up," I cringed, lowering my head and chuckling.

"I love it when you blush," he remarked, as the laughter turned to chuckles.

"I don't!" I chuckled back. "I'm forever doing it... it gives the game away."

"It highlights your beauty." He smiled softly.

I sighed. "You know what? This is going to happen, isn't it?" I impatiently asked.

David's eyes darted from one side of the room to the other. "What is?"

"Us sleeping together again."

David nearly choked on his champagne. "Bloody hell, El!" He laughed, trying to swallow the mouthful he had and wiping his chin. "You do know how to come out with things!"

"It's the truth." I grinned. "We're here, all this flirting and what not... but we both know what we want."

"We do? I thought I did, but then you threw me off with the random job offer. And last night... well, you practically booted me out of your house afterwards!" He smiled. "It's not the impression you gave off that you wanted to do it again. I don't actually know where I stand with you."

"I want some fun. I don't want anything serious, and I want it to be kept between us, and us only. I'm tired of rejection and people walking out on me, but we both have needs that can be fulfilled. We do have good sex, and you're not bad to look at." I winked.

"Oh well, that's a compliment if ever I received one." David smiled. "But, El, it's just so not like you."

"Good!' I stated sternly. "I'm fed up of being like me! I work too hard, I try to maintain relationships, but end up being crapped on half of the time!"

"Well, that's something I definitely won't do to you," he joked. "But why me, El? I can't believe I am actually questioning this... I must need my head testing, again... but you could have any man you wanted."

"Could I?" I wondered out loud, thinking back to Brandon. "I suppose I'm comfortable with you, even though I never thought I would be again. You know me, you know my body, and I know yours. It's just a physical thing that I need. I don't want a relationship, and if I met someone else, there's half a chance they'd want something like that. We both know where we stand."

"Okay, fine. I won't object to that." He grinned and then paused for a second. "So do you want to do it now, then? Or talk first? Now I don't know what to do with myself... I'm in uncharted waters here." He laughed.

"We need to unwind. That conversation has made things awkward." I thought for a moment. "I know... let's go for a swim."

"A swim? El, you're becoming more random by the minute. You want me to be your swim coach or something?" He chuckled.

I rolled my eyes. "Not helping. We have a pool house next to the downstairs gym. I hardly ever use it. But we could take this bottle and just unwind in there. I don't want a quick grope on the sofa again. Plus, Penny found the rubber packet when she was cleaning up."

David burst out laughing. "Oh dear lord! I bet she nearly keeled over when she found it!"

"She's been very diplomatic about it and actually hasn't mentioned anything. It was Roger who told me, because he was with her."

"Roger?! Oh geez, if he's found out, then good luck keeping this a secret, El."

"No, no. He's very good... he won't say anything. Anyway, this conversation is killing my libido. Let's go."

Grabbing the bottle and my glass, David followed on behind me with his glass in hand. I couldn't believe I was walking with David, through into the pool house, to go and have sex with him - this was so bizarre. I never really used the pool house; I was always too busy anyway, and there was no way I was sleeping with David in my bed where I had been with Stephen.

Stepping into the pool house, I flicked on a couple of the wall lights to give off a slight glow so we could see where we were going. I placed the bottle and glass down on a small table at the side of the pool, and grinned at David as I started to undress. He smiled back and followed suit, placing his glass down and then removing his clothing.

Without a blink, David dove gracefully into the pool and under the water, as I watched his stunning physique beneath the ripple of the warm blue liquid. He then resurfaced a bit further away.

"Coming in?" he called over while smiling - his gorgeous blond waves drenched and swept back on his head.

Doing the same, I dove into the water. Further ahead I could see David's body waiting for me, so I swam underwater until I reached him. Resurfacing just before him, my auburn hair now wet through and swept back in the same fashion, David wrapped his arms around me. This was like when I'd first met him; that beautiful man who I knew could easily have been a model. He looked like he was in a photoshoot for a swimsuit collection - except for there was no swimsuit - and I thought that there was no better person to be fooling around with.

He slid his arms around my body under the water and leant down and kissed me, with the beads of water slowly ebbing their way down our faces. I wrapped my legs around his waist, as he backed me onto the side of the pool. Moving in a motion which sent the water rippling backwards and forwards around us, I reached my arms out wide onto the sides of the pool and gripped the edge. Leaning my head back, he kissed my neck, sending sensations ripping straight through me.

The feel of the water massaging my body at the same time was sensational, and we both exploded with an intense euphoria at the end. Kissing each other once more and then parting our bodies, we both swam to the other side of the pool where we had left our drinks, and sipped our champagne.

"Well, that wasn't what I thought I would be doing tonight." He smiled.

"What were you going to be doing?" I asked, leaning my arms on the side of the pool and watching him.

"Dinner and a movie, perhaps. But believe me, that was so much better." He grinned.

"Nothing like a bit of skinny dipping." I winked.

"That wasn't your average skinny dip." He laughed. "When do you want to see me again?" he asked, looking at me with those cool blue eyes.

"I'll call you," I leisurely replied.

"Fair enough." He smirked, pushing himself up on the side of the pool to get out.

I watched on as he wandered over to the corner of the pool house to get a towel from the neatly folded stack in the corner. He was a lovely sight if ever there was one, and completely naked and walking with such ease, I could've watched him all night.

Deciding that I'd better get out of the pool myself, I swam over to the steps, as there was no way I could haul myself out without looking like a beach whale that had been washed up. Emerging from the water, I walked over to him as he was drying himself and grabbed a towel. I stopped as I was dabbing my hair with it, due to David standing and staring at me.

"What?" I asked, wondering why he was staring.

"Nothing. I just thought I would take in the view, because whenever you call this arrangement off with us, I want to remember how beautiful you are with no clothes on." He gently smiled, before continuing to dress himself.

Smiling to myself, I dressed and then showed David to the door. The most unexpected encounters in the world were happening with him, and I was still struck by how unbelievable this all was.

He turned as he got to the front door, leaning over and placing a soft kiss on my cheek.

"Night, El," he softly whispered, as he opened the door and made his way out.

Closing the front door behind him, I leant back on it. For all of his flaws and past mistakes, he was the one person who had made me feel good right now, and no matter what, I was going to enjoy it.

I DID FIND THAT I HAD a spring in my step the next day, and it felt good to be in control of my life. I was a rich, successful woman, and from now on, it was my way or no way. I never thought in a million years that it would have been David that would be the turning point for me to feel this way, but he was providing me with what I needed at present - good sex on tap.

Penny had been right about one thing; if I tackled one problem at a time, every scenario would soon resolve itself. One of the problems I had was a lack of fun. Most nights I could be found sitting around the house like some nun - and that needed to change.

When I received a text from Darcy, asking whether I wanted to go out that night, I jumped at the chance. I wanted to get myself out there, as I was newly single-ish, and definitely ready to mingle. It would be nice to spend an evening with someone who was also single and up for having fun. Darcy held no punches and was also ready to embrace life, and I figured that it would be nice to be around some like-minded company.

That evening when I got home from work, I spent some time with the children and then went and got myself ready for a big night out. Donning a sexy little dress and heels, I felt good about myself, and that's the way things were going to stay.

Penny and Roger seemed happy that I was getting out and about. They were the ones that were constantly subjected to me moping at home, so to see me up and about and being my usual happy self, they were pleased for me. I didn't need a man in my life, because let's face it, they all wanted something. I never really needed anything from them, apart from the odd session, as I was pretty self-sufficient. There were definitely perks to being over thirty - I was in control of my life, and due to the mistakes I made in my twenties, I knew what I never wanted to happen again.

At 7pm, Darcy was at the door ready for our night out.

"Hi, Eleanor!" she greeted. "Aw, I'm so pleased you said you would come out tonight! Come on, the car's waiting."

She smiled my way, and I closed the front door behind me to make my way down the steps. Darcy had hired a car for us to travel in, and I was excited about where we would be going. Settling in the backseat of the car, she turned to me.

"So, how are you? Anything new occurring?" She smiled, with her dark eyes glinting away.

"No, nothing new," I lied - I wasn't even about to mention to her that I was sleeping with her brother. "I'm looking forward to having some fun for a change. Where are we going tonight?"

"I thought we'd try somewhere different. It's a bar where there's loads of cute guys. I thought it would be fun. I knew you needed some cheering up." She grinned.

"You're right. I need to let my hair down. I'm fed up of sitting home alone each night." I chuckled.

"You're in good company." She winked.

Being driven along, Darcy poured us each a glass of champagne that was available to us in the car, as we chatted about what I was up to at work with the expansion, and how life generally was with her. It was nice to let my hair down with some female company. I'd had years of missing out on things like this, and it was time to make up for it.

As the car pulled over, I peered out of the window to see where we had stopped. I looked up at the bar which looked like it could really use a lick of paint. Motorcycles lined the outside, and yeah, I'd never been there before. It was called Huskies, and was in a real deadbeat part of town. These were definitely circles that I didn't move in.

"Are we going in here?" I wondered, still staring open-mouthed out of the window.

"Yeah, it'll be fun!" Darcy smiled.

"But, Darcy, this place is full of unsavoury types," I muttered.

"No it's not! You read too much into stereotypes. They're all pussy cats under the stern leather exterior." She smirked, as the chauffeur opened the door for her, and she stepped out.

The chauffeur was next to let me out, and I could feel eyes on us as we got out of the car. The bikers inside were probably looking at us and wondering what the hell we were doing there.

"I'm not sure about this," I spoke, feeling really out of place in my little sexy dress.

"Oh, come on, live a little." Darcy chuckled, grabbing hold of my hand and practically dragging me inside the bar. "You'll feel better once you get a drink inside of you."

Reluctantly walking in behind Darcy, I was right - we did stand out. Inside, there were lots of tattooed bikers wearing leather garments, with the odd rough and ready woman looking our way. The place seemed to come to a standstill as everyone looked our way as we walked in. It was quite busy, with the faint buzz of jukebox music in the background.

Darcy didn't seem phased, as she walked in with her head held high, and straight up to the bar.

"Two whiskeys on the rocks, bartender," she purred over to the guy who was wiping a glass and eyeing us intently.

I must have looked like I'd seen a ghost, as I stood there wide-eyed and not sure how to move. Slowly, the bikers seemed to edge back to their business of whatever they were doing, and I was relieved not to be getting stared at. Darcy turned to me and handed me my drink. I took a sip and it was really strong. I wasn't used to drinking things like whiskey, and usually preferred something a little less potent.

"Do you come to this bar a lot?" I wondered as I slurped my drink, wishing it was a cosmopolitan.

"Sometimes. It depends, really. I like to mix up what class of people I drink with. Plus I like a man in leather." She smiled.

"Fair enough. I've never actually been in a place like this before."

"The key is to loosen up and have fun. If you look defensive, then that causes trouble. People here just want to have a good night. They don't want to be bothered."

"Ah okay," I replied, drinking some more of my whiskey.

A couple of drinks later, and we were happily sat at the bar and enjoying each other's company. More people had started to pile in, and the place was bustling with people chilling out and having a good time. Darcy got up and put a song on over the jukebox, as she started to sway her hips and dance along in front of where we were sitting.

"Come on, Eleanor! Have a dance!" she cheered.

Considering I wasn't comfortable when I'd first walked in, I was feeling pretty mellow now after a few drinks, so I got up and joined her. We danced around each other, swaying our hips and dancing a little more seductively than I usually would, but I was following Darcy's lead.

Before long, there were a few men standing around us, cheering us on and clapping and whooping, as we seemed to be taken away by both the atmosphere and the several whiskeys we'd been downing. After a while, my feet started to ache through the numbing sensation of the alcohol, and I wanted a breather. Propping myself on the bar stool, in a very unladylike manner, the room swirled around me.

"I'm going to the bathroom!" Darcy shouted over the music and chattering that was going on around us.

"Okay!" I drunkenly smiled at her.

Watching her wander over to the ladies restroom, I swiveled myself around and ordered a water from the bartender. The bartender looked amused, as he leisurely filled a glass of water up for me and slid it over the counter in my direction. I took a big glug of it and it was refreshing to taste. It served to both hydrate, and wake me up a little, as I could have easily gone to sleep.

As I sat on the stool, practically slumped over the bar, I felt someone near my side.

"Hey, pretty lady," the voice came, as I turned my head to see that it was one of the guys who had been watching us dancing earlier on.

"Hey," I leisurely replied, not really interested in his attention, and wanting to sip my water.

"What's a pretty lady like you, doing in a bar like this?" he asked, as he slid himself onto the seat next to me.

I rolled my eyes at perhaps the lamest pick-up line in the world. "I'm here with a friend," I bluntly replied.

"Oh yeah... you mean the friend that's leaving now?" He smirked.

The guy nodded toward the door, and as I looked over, I could see Darcy exiting on the arm of some random guy. Oh great, was she leaving me here? How was I going to get home? I stood up from the bar stool, grabbing my purse, and was just about to bolt over to Darcy and ask her what the hell she was doing.

As I stood up and was about to walk away, I felt someone grip my arm, and I turned to find it was the guy who had been sat next to me.

"Where are you going?" He grinned, pulling me into him.

"Home," I snapped.

"Oh no you're not. I thought you and me could have some fun," he leered at me, with the stale stench of beer on his breath.

This would've been a great time to sober up. I pressed my hands into his chest, as I fought to push him away as he was trying to bring his face in toward mine. His hands were around my waist, and I felt sick at his touch.

"Get off me!" I shouted over the noise in the bar, as I struggled to get him away.

"You know you want it. You've been egging me on all night," he sneered.

"I have not! Now get off me!" I squirmed trying to desperately get out of his grasp.

"You need to be taught a good, *hard* lesson," he fumed as I tried to break free.

Feeling the sick swirl in my stomach, I fought to get him away. It was no use; he had a death grip on me, and I wasn't strong enough to fight him off.

"Hands off the lady!" a voice boomed behind him.

He stopped trying to contain me in his grasp and turned around. I looked behind the sleazy guy's shoulder, and saw none other than Brandon standing there.

"And you are?" the guy sneered, turning his attention from me to Brandon, as I stood there like a rabbit caught in headlights.

"A friend... not that it's any of your concern who I am," Brandon sternly replied, overpowering the man with his presence.

The guy walked right up to Brandon, and a few inches shorter, he struggled to square up to him in his eyeline.

"You and me, outside... right now," the guy threatened.

"You really don't want to be offering me that," Brandon grinned.

"Outside. Now," the guy hissed.

Brandon silently walked around him, nodding at me and heading for the door, with the creepy guy practically foaming at the mouth and following him outside. I felt rooted to the spot, but I knew I had to move. If Brandon lost this fight, what was going to happen then? I'd be stranded here with this loser, and goodness-knows-what would occur. I had to at least try and help him in some way.

I quickly hobbled on behind them, ignoring anyone else in the bar as I fought my way through. I swung open the door of the bar and felt the cool night air hit my face. Stepping outside, I looked around to witness the sight of Brandon and this guy standing in the parking lot, a few feet apart, and ready to fight.

Before I could make my way further toward them, the guy lunged toward Brandon, and swung at him. Brandon swerved his punch with pure ease, and then seemed to go in for the attack. He immediately hit him back, knocking him back and nearly launching him onto the floor. Wide-eyed, I watched on, as the guy composed himself, holding his jaw in his hands and his face filling with rage. He lunged toward Brandon again, as Brandon grabbed hold of his hand, twisting it around and getting his arm up his back. The man's face creased in pain as he was stood there immobilized in Brandon's grip.

"Enough!" I shouted, as I staggered over in my heels toward where Brandon was. "Just let him go."

Brandon looked at me with his green eyes ablaze with fury, as he noted the pleading look on my face and reluctantly pushed him away.

"She's not worth it anyway!" the guy spat, in pain and with a bruised ego, as he shot back in the bar and out of sight.

Brandon turned to me. "Home, now," he fumed, as he grabbed my hand and pulled me toward a Harley that was parked out front.

"Is this yours?" I wondered, eyeing the sleek motorcycle that was parked there.

"Yes, now get this on and hurry up. He's probably gone back in there to get the rest of them." He shoved a helmet my way and I quickly put it on.

Trying to desperately get on the back of it in a mini-dress, my underwear was definitely on show. I didn't care - I wanted out of this place. I clung on, still feeling the remnants of the whiskey in my stomach, as I wrapped my arms around Brandon's waist and he sped off down the road and away from the run-down dump.

Quickly looked behind, Brandon was right - a group of bikers had now emerged from the bar, and were looking around the parking lot for Brandon - the sleazeball that was trying it on with me, leading the way.

A while later, we arrived back at my house. He climbed off the motorcycle, and I swayed as I tried to unhook my leg and get my balance back - trying desperately to maintain a little bit of dignity in this stupid dress.

"Here, let me help you," Brandon offered, helping me leverage my leg from around the seat.

"I'm fine," I protested, as I eventually got off it and stood up, fixing my dress back down and into place.

"What the hell were you doing in that place?" He frowned, watching me mess about with my clothing.

"None of your business," I snapped, frustrated with this damn skirt.

"I think it is when something like that happens and I have to step in," he snapped back.

"Listen..." I stood up straight and faced him, "I appreciate you defending me, but I didn't ask for you to step in. It's not like I called you up and asked for your help." I rifled around in my purse for my key, as I made my way to the front door.

"I didn't mean it like that," Brandon started, following me on behind. "It's just that place is a complete dive... you shouldn't have been alone in there."

Placing the key in the lock, I made my way through the front door. Kicking off my shoes, I placed my purse down as Brandon stood in the doorway.

"For your information, I wasn't alone. I was with a friend," I stated.

"Well, where was this 'friend'?" he asked, leaning against the door frame.

I lowered my head. "She left with some guy."

"Oh, that sounds like a great friend, leaving you alone in there!" He fumed.

"Darcy's fine. I think we'd had too much to drink."

"That's a given. I think half of the guys in there could see that as well."

"Like I said, thank you for your help and getting me out of there. But my friends and where I go is really none of your concern." I swayed, as I realized I hadn't sobered up as much as I would have liked.

"No, it's not. But try and chose your friends wisely." Brandon turned and walked away from me. Just as he was about to mount his Harley, he turned back. "And drink some water." He smirked, placing his helmet on, revving the engine, and riding away.

Sighing, I shut the door behind me, still feeling the wobble of being drunk in my legs. Dragging my tired body along, I wandered upstairs and got into my bedroom. I couldn't even be bothered to undress, so I slumped onto my bed, face first, and fell fast asleep.

I AWOKE IN THE MORNING, with a disgusting taste in my mouth, as I peeled my face off the pillow it was stuck to. Slowly getting up, the pounding in my head overtook any other feeling. I felt sick as well, and with the ache behind my eyes, I couldn't even bear the thought of moving.

"Miss. Eleanor!" Penny shouted outside of the door. "You're going to be late for work! I have some breakfast for you!"

I slumped myself on the edge of the bed. "Penny, could you call Clarisse and tell her I'm not going in," I called out, trying not to talk too loudly.

"Are you ill, child?" she called through the door.

"Nothing serious," I replied. "I just need to rest. I'll come down for breakfast soon."

"Okay!" she called back to me, and I could hear the shuffle of her footsteps move away from the door.

Carefully laying back down on the bed, the room swirled - what a night that was. I felt sick when I thought about that horrible whiskey I'd been drinking. It tasted like lavatory cleaner - well, whatever that may have tasted like.

Hauling myself up, I realized that I was still in my dress from last night. I slowly plodded toward my walk-in wardrobe and found something comfy to wear. I definitely wasn't going into work today, and a t-shirt and jeans would suit me just fine. Grabbing a quick shower, it did help to ebb the flow of the hangover that was raging through my body.

I knew I had to eat and drink something, as I was dehydrated after last night, and what a night it had been. I thought back to being with Darcy, and dancing with her. I didn't like the way she had left me there and gone off with some random male. I wouldn't have dreamt of doing that to a friend I was with. It wasn't safe to be doing that to someone, so I wouldn't be going on anymore nights out with her again anytime soon.

Wandering into the kitchen, I slowly grazed on a piece of toast, which didn't seem to sit too well on my stomach. I did enjoy the fresh orange I was drinking, though, and sipping that seemed to help. Penny seemed amused by my presence in the kitchen this morning. She wasn't stupid, and knew I wasn't ill - I was majorly hungover.

As I sat at the table, my cell in my pocket buzzed - it was Darcy:
Great night last night, Eleanor. We'll have to do it again soon! x
Yeah, that wasn't going to happen, but I knew that I had to text her back to not seem rude.

I replied:
Yeah, I had fun. Where did you go? x
Moments later her reply came:
Hooked up with some guy. Wasn't worth it in the end. Speak to you soon x
Oh right, so no asking how I was, or how I got home? Yeah, I wasn't particularly impressed with that behavior. I liked my friends to be loyal, and that wasn't loyalty at all.

Placing my cell back in my pocket, I made the journey into the living room. Today I was going to put my feet up and watch crap daytime TV until this hangover decided to go away. Thankfully, Penny had provided me with a pitcher of lemon water in the living area, and while I couldn't force any food down, that was definitely the safest bet.

Journeying to the living room, I was stopped in my tracks by the doorbell ringing. I was praying it wasn't Darcy with another dodgy plan, but she would have had to have gotten around to the house in a flash, since texting me a couple of minutes ago. I reluctantly opened the door, as the stream of sunshine flooded in, and I squinted to see who was stood there.

"Good morning, sunshine!" Brandon smiled.

"Not so loud," I replied in a hushed tone.

He laughed and removed his sunglasses, stepping through the door. "I thought I would come round and see if you were okay this morning." He chuckled. "It's plain to see, that you are indeed, suffering from the dreaded hangover."

"Hmm..." I mumbled, as I headed off to sit down in the living room, with Brandon following on behind.

He took a seat on the recliner, while I slumped on the sofa, leaning back with my hand on my head.

"Well, this is riveting." He chuckled, remarking on the lack of conversation taking place.

"Brandon, I don't mean to sound rude, but what do you want?" I impatiently asked.

He laughed again - I winced at the sound.

"I did come by to see how you were after last night," he began.

"Yeah, thank you for getting me out of there. It was a dump, and I'm never going back." I sighed.

"Good to hear. Lesson learnt." He grinned. "But anyway, I was also wondering if you fancied coming to a function with me tonight?"

"The thought of leaving the house..." I grumbled - eyes still closed and leaning back on the sofa.

"The effects of whatever it was you were drinking last night will have worn off by then." He chuckled. "Anyway, this function is at 8pm tonight. I thought you may relish the chance to be out on the town?"

I thought back to my new-and-improved-me plan, and how I wanted more of a social life now that I was free and single.

Opening my eyes, I squinted over at him. "Yeah, okay. But what function is it? And why do you want to take me?" I wondered.

"Because I was serious when I said I wanted to be friends. I do like you and I enjoy your company... when you're not drunk or hungover." He chuckled. "It's a work thing, there may be some good contacts for you there. It's at a venue where there will be free drinks and food... that's all I go for. Plus I thought it would be good for you to be around the nicer people of society." He smirked.

"True." I sighed. "Yes, count me in. It would be nice to be out this evening for a change."

"Great." Brandon grinned, standing up. "I'll pick you up at half-seven. Just a cocktail dress will be required. And don't worry, I'll get you virgin cocktails again... no more liquor for you, young lady." He laughed.

"Thanks, Dad." I lightly laughed back, still feeling the throb in my head.

Brandon placed his sunglasses on and left the house - the faint click of the front door closing behind him. I did like Brandon, and even though I could've cringed for the way I'd thrown myself at him that night, I liked being around him. Another thing was that I knew I was safe in his company. After last night, he had certainly proven that to me. He could not only take care of himself, but he had moves that could take down anyone around who was a nuisance, and that was good enough for me. His behavior spoke volumes, which was in stark contrast to Darcy. Brandon was definitely a friend that I liked to have around.

Filling my glass with lemon water, I sat back as I took a sip, thinking over Brandon's invitation to a function tonight. I also thought about him stood there in his sunglasses looking super cool this morning - he always dressed so well.

Then there was his wicked sense of humor and dance moves, which would make for a good night tonight. I sat back as it then dawned on me why he had knocked me back. Maybe I wasn't as unattractive as I first thought?

Brandon was gay.

Chapter Eight - The Dating Game

I'd had a fairly normal day at home. Clarisse had called me to see if I was okay, and I did explain to her that I'd gone out and drank too much the previous night. She actually laughed when I told her that. The reason I did tell her was to put her mind at ease, as so much had happened lately, and I didn't want her to think anything was seriously wrong.

Knowing all was running well at work, I proceeded to feel my hangover ebb slowly away, as I basically slobbed about and did nothing. Natalie had collected the twins from school and was busy collecting Henry from Kindergarten, so I'd had a peaceful day.

After dinner, I took myself off to my bedroom to get ready for the night ahead. I remembered Brandon telling me that I needed a cocktail dress, so I dug out a sparkly blue one and placed it on. Checking out my reflection in the floor-length mirror, a hint of sadness came across me, as I imagined the reflection of Stephen, watching me getting ready from behind. He would always pass a compliment as I was getting dressed, and it was little things like that, that I did miss.

Pulling myself together, I placed my shoes on and grabbed a purse to match - I couldn't think like that anymore. I ventured down to the salon to find Roger, who I'd asked to get me looking glam and ready for tonight. He was as thrilled as ever to oblige, and by the time he was finished, I looked like the hangover I'd been suffering from all day didn't even exist.

Thanking him, I checked my cell in my bag - it was now seven-thirty. Bang on time, Brandon was at the door and waiting to collect me.

"Wow!" He smiled when he saw me. "You look fantastic!"

"Thank you. You look very handsome in your tux." I smiled back.

Brandon chuckled and held his arm out for me to link, as he escorted me to the car that he had arrived in. Seated comfortably in the back, we chatted happily about what Brandon had been doing today, and what the function was in aid of. It was for an old friend of Brandon's who had just merged his business with another firm, and was keen to celebrate. It was always nice to be attending something happy, so I was glad he had asked me to come along.

Brandon told me that his friend was looking for a design company to take over for a new look for their merging companies, and he had told him about me. I was very flattered that Brandon had thought of me, and due to that he must've been impressed with the work that we were carrying out for his corporation.

When we arrived at the venue, it was all glitz and glamor. Tonnes of people were entering through the doors, dressed in their finest, and it was in stark contrast to where I had ended up last night. Spotlights flashed inside, and the spill of music poured out onto the street. People seemed to be in high spirits and I was keen to join them. The chauffeur opened the door, and Brandon got out first, reaching back inside to take my hand.

As I stepped out of the vehicle, I took his arm, as he leisurely waved to a few people around him, who then eyed me - probably wondering who I was. We walked in and were met by a sea of people, sometimes interrupted by the waiting staff who were walking in between and giving out glasses of champagne. As the tray was offered to us, I took a glass. I was only having this one tonight - another hangover tomorrow was something that I didn't need.

We milled about the crowd, and Brandon greeted a few faces that were familiar to him. I did recognize a couple of the guests, and they politely waved to me. Music played, drinks and appetizers were being served, and the atmosphere was both busy and lovely at the same time. Brandon leant in a few times to me to explain who other people were, and I found him to be a big help. If I was going to be talking to some people, then it helped to know what company they were a part of.

Soon switching to my virgin cocktails, the one glass of champagne I was drinking was taking affect. It was definitely topping off the alcohol that was still in my bloodstream after last night. After more schmoozing, Brandon stopped near to a group who were stood near the bar, and turned to talk to me.

"This is where you come in. My friend, Rob, is with this group of people. He's the guy who I've being telling you about, who is throwing this bash tonight."

"Great." I smiled. "Let's go and speak to him."

Brandon smiled back at me and then politely interrupted the group of people that were talking near to us. A couple of the people stood in front of us parted, so we could be let into the circle.

"Brandon, my man! Glad you could make it!"

Brandon laughed. "Rob, nice to see you again... great party. I brought the lady who I was telling you about. She owns Rose Designs, and they are doing a fantastic job for my company at the moment." Brandon turned to me. "Eleanor, this is Rob, Rob, Eleanor," he introduced.

"Nice to meet you, Rob," I replied, politely placing my hand out for him to shake.

"Eleanor, a pleasure indeed," he replied, taking my hand and gently kissing the back of it.

Rob smiled at me and pulled away. I watched on as he continued to talk about something to whomever it was that was around him, and then made his excuses to end that particular conversation. I watched him as he spoke - he was nice to observe. He was refined, about six-feet, with broad shoulders and a lovely smile. With dark brown hair and bright blue eyes, he did stand out from the crowd. After a moment, he broke away from who he was with, and ushered me and Brandon to join him a bit further away.

"Sorry about that." He smiled toward me. "I just had to deal with a bit of business with those people. Anyway, Eleanor, Brandon has been telling me all about the wonderful work you have been doing for Brandon Corporation."

"That's very kind of him." I smiled toward Brandon, before turning back to Rob. "But it's no more than I would put into any business. One hundred percent the whole way." I grinned. "We are expanding at the moment, so we must be doing something right."

"Sounds interesting. I am really interested in talking more about this to you." Rob grinned back.

"If you both will excuse me, I have just seen someone I need to talk to," Brandon interrupted. "I'll leave you in Rob's capable hands for now."

"No worries. See you in a bit," I replied.

Brandon walked away while I stood with Rob and we continued to talk.

"So, Rob, Brandon tells me that your company is merging with another?" I began.

"Yes, we've been very blessed indeed. It's all about bringing everything together to merge both ends of success. It's set to be both lucrative and satisfying." He smiled.

"Sounds good. I bet you can't wait," I replied.

"Hmm..." Rob took a sip of his drink. "I'll be glad when it's all done. I've been working too hard lately, and could do with a break."

"You and me both." I chuckled in agreement.

Rob paused for a moment, scanning my face. "I hope you don't think me forward, but would you like to have dinner with me tomorrow?"

"Oh, erm..." I mumbled, totally thrown off-guard.

"Ah, don't worry. I gather you're married. All the beautiful ladies are always taken." He smirked.

"No, no. Well, I am, but we are separated. It's a very long story which I won't bore you with." I smiled. "Dinner would be lovely. We could talk business if you like?"

"That is one subject that I would like to cover. But I would like to take you out, anyway, if that's okay?"

"Like on a date?" I gasped.

"Yes." He chuckled. "I don't know why you seem so surprised at me asking you."

I blushed slightly. "It's very quick... and we may be working together."

"Doesn't matter." He grinned. "I believe in taking the bull by the horns... live life to the fullest, and if you like something, then go for it. I already know how much I like you, and Brandon speaks very highly of you. I trust his opinion immensely."

"That's sweet," I shyly replied. "I'm gathering you are referring to me as the bull?" I laughed.

Rob laughed. "As much as I do see that what I said could be construed that way... you are most definitely a swan. But there is no saying that I can think of about life that involves one of them."

"True. I can't think of anything. So what time tomorrow?" I wondered, eyeing him curiously.

"About 7pm? With your permission, I will get your address from Brandon, to pick you up."

"7pm is perfect. Yes, by all means... Brandon knows all too well where I live." I smirked.

"Meaning?" Rob wondered.

"Nothing." I shook my head and smiled. "It's just in a short space of time he has been to my house, sometimes under some unexpected circumstances."

"I'm curious to know what you are talking about. You'll have to tell me over dinner tomorrow." He grinned.

"Some things I don't even think I could bring myself to repeat. But we will talk tomorrow."

"I'm intrigued, Eleanor. Brandon was right on that." He smirked.

"On what?" I eyed.

"That you are a woman of mystery. I'm not sure why he said that to me, but I'm sure there's a valid reason for it. Brandon doesn't mince his words. Still waters run deep?" He winked.

I wasn't sure whether he was talking about me or Brandon at this point, so I thought it best to swerve answering the question. Just as Rob was about to say something else, Brandon came back over to us, breaking up our conversation.

"Can I steal her back now?" Brandon grinned.

"Reluctantly, yes." Rob smiled my way. "Brandon, could I have a word for a moment?"

"Of course," he replied.

Rob pulled Brandon to one side, out of earshot of me, as a few words were exchanged, and a few glances from Brandon were shot my way. I gathered that he was perhaps asking Brandon for my address, but I couldn't gauge what was going on in his head through his expressions. I felt kind of awkward stood there - like when you were asking your friend to go and ask a boy whether he liked you. But I couldn't move off anywhere else because I didn't know anyone that well, and I'd been invited to this function as a guest. A moment or so later, Rob left Brandon's presence, and Brandon came back over to me.

"Everything okay?" I wondered, having an inclination of what had been said, but not knowing what Brandon was thinking.

"A-ha," Brandon bluntly replied, looking around the room and seeming a little annoyed.

"You don't seem okay," I stated.

"What?" Brandon seemed to snap back to attention. "No, no. I'm fine, come on, let's get another drink."

He took my hand and that was that line of questioning over. I wasn't sure what that reaction was about, but I wasn't going there. They could have been talking about anything, and it wasn't my place to pry.

After a few more drinks, we got chatting to more people, and Brandon seemed to be in fine fettle again, as he whirled me around the dancefloor that people were heading to when they had some Dutch courage inside of them. Dancing to "Respect" by Erasure, Brandon was whirling me around and mimicking the words to me, as I danced in front of him and laughed. It was quite apt, though, as all's I'd wanted over the past few weeks was some respect, and Brandon had provided me with more than the illusive husband had in ages. It was a real pity that Brandon was attracted to men, although I did look upon him as being a good friend now, and all romantic notions were nicely wearing off.

When the clock struck midnight, scared of me turning into a pumpkin, Brandon had me safely dropped off at home, after a lovely, but tiring, night.

"Thanks so much for inviting me tonight." I turned and smiled to him as we sat in the car.

"It's been a pleasure having you with me. You brightened up what otherwise could have been a fairly dull experience." He smiled back.

"I don't know... I think there was a lot of nice people there tonight," I thought back.

"Hmm, Rob in particular, by any chance?" he wondered.

"He was a nice man. But I was talking about a few others that we spoke to as well... including the present company in this car." I gently smiled.

As I was just about to get out of the car, Brandon placed his hand on my arm. "Eleanor, are you going on a date with Rob tomorrow evening?" he asked.

I swirled my head around to face him. "I'm not sure if you would label it as a date, but yes, I'm going out for dinner with him. Why?"

"No reason. Rob is okay. It's just you're still married, and I didn't think it was like you to go on dates when it's not been that long since your husband left. First the bar, now this. Correct me if I'm wrong, but is this really like you?"

I narrowed my eyes at him - I had only known him five minutes, but whether he had a good read on me or not, was it really his place to ask me those questions?

I turned back in the seat of the car to face him. "Listen, Brandon, I appreciate your concern... if that's what this is... but you don't know me that well yet. I'm thankful for you saving me at that bar, but to be asking me whether I should be going on a date or not... is that really any of your business?"

"It is when I think you're on the rebound," Brandon bluntly stated.

I shook my head in confusion. "Brandon, you are not interested in me, which is fine because I like us being friends, but just because you aren't, what makes you so sure that no other man would be and that I would not take them up on the offer of dinner? I'm not going to sit around at home and wait for a man who clearly doesn't want to be with me anymore. And to be fair, we have only known each other for a short amount of time, so why are you so bothered about these things?"

"I'm not," Brandon protested. "It's just, even though we have only known each other a short space of time, I do care about you, and I wouldn't want you to get hurt."

"That's fair enough, but my love life is generally my business. I don't know the first thing about yours... although I have an idea."

"You do?" Brandon eyed.

"Well, yeah... you're gay, right?"

Brandon smirked and turned to face his driver. "Goodnight, Eleanor."

Baffled by the expression, I got out of the car and made my way to the front door. Brandon watched on as I safely entered the house, and gave me a little wave as he was driven away. I waved back and then closed the front door behind me. I didn't think I was certain of anything anymore, except for one thing - people were strange.

WORK WAS THE USUAL bustle the next day, and the building that we were expanding to was set to be ready in little less than a weeks' time. It wouldn't be fully opening then, as there was still the issue of staffing to sort, which I was partially relying on Caroline for. I'd seen Jeanie at work, and apart from her discussing some design issues with me, she hadn't mentioned Stephen.

I was definitely now numb where he was concerned, and to be fair, I didn't want to think about him. I wanted to carry on with my life, and not be burdened with thoughts about what he could be up to.

Texting David about when the new premises would be finished, he informed me that he was working his notice at Jefferson's, and would be free to join us in a couple of weeks' time. I think he was edging for an invite to my house tonight, but of course it was my date with Rob, so I was busy playing the field. I quite liked being in control and having my options open. I'd gone from being rejected, to being in demand, and I was in my element.

I felt much lighter and carefree knowing that things at work were due to settle down soon, and that home-life was actually running smoothly and making me happy. When I had a moment, me and Clarisse had put our heads together and were arranging a big celebration bash for the expansion, at a swanky hotel in town called Paradise Palms. It was a beautiful venue, and the hotel was top notch. The gardens around it were also fabulous, and I was arranging a night that would be themed as black and white. It would all be upper class, as I was settling for nothing less lately, especially after me having a taste of the less finer things in life with Darcy.

The people around me who I did still class as family, people such as Jeanie and Tasha, I wanted to be at the event, as they were the people who had supported the business in some way or another. Considering David wasn't with us just yet, I had invited him, as Caroline had expressed to me that there was no time like the present to start 'keeping an eye on him'. Little did she know how much I was actually keeping on him at the moment.

Talking of Caroline, she was inviting some of the wealthiest people that she knew, so I had to go all out for this event whether I liked it or not. A few special clients that the business had catered for were coming along as well - some of the rich and famous - so the media were expected to be outside, to take some shots of whomever it was that was entering the building. This would considerably lift the profile of Rose Designs, and I wanted the world to know how well the business was doing.

I was so excited when I thought about it. It would be a night filled with some of the most wonderful people in my life, and some of the greatest contacts in the world. I could have almost skipped around work thinking about it. The excitement was like that of being a child again, and it was great.

But, first things first, and when I finished my working day, I had to quickly venture home to be ready on time for my dinner with Rob. I was looking forward to seeing him again. He was handsome and seemed to be a nice man, so it was going to be lovely to be wined and dined for the evening by him. Penny knew of my plans, so didn't make dinner for me, and of course, Roger was on hand to make me look my ultimate best.

Dressed in a satin, cream, floor-length dress, I felt really good. I placed a diamond necklace on, and felt like the belle of the ball. My confidence was back, and nothing was going to shake it this time.

At 7pm, Rob arrived to collect me, carrying a beautiful bouquet of red roses in his arms.

"Oh, they are lovely!" I beamed as he handed them to me at the door.

"Only the best for such a beautiful lady." He smiled.

"Thank you." I smiled back, feeling my cheeks heat up at the compliment.

As I turned around, Penny was stood behind me. She smiled, nodded, and took them from me. She was wonderful, and was always there at the right time.

Rob took my hand and guided me out of the door and down the steps to his car which was waiting for us. It was a black limousine, and was very nice indeed. It was like a bar in itself inside, and with the comfiest leather interior I'd sat on in ages, it was a miniature haven.

"How are you today?" he asked, handing me a glass of champagne.

I took the glass from him and smirked to myself when I thought about how I was fast in danger of becoming an alcoholic at this rate.

"Fine, thank you. You?" I asked, taking a sip of the golden liquid.

"Good, yes. All the better for seeing you tonight. You look absolutely radiant," he beamed.

"Thank you." I blushed.

"No need to be embarrassed about your own beauty," he remarked. "It amazes me how some of the most stunning ladies I have ever been around, really don't know how beautiful they truly are. Some of the less... how do I phrase this? Less facially fortunate, always think they are wonderful." He chuckled.

"That's an awful thing to say!" I laughed, trying not to laugh a little too hard at the statement.

"I'm nothing, if not honest, Eleanor. I speak the truth. Which is why I have done so well in business."

"So what exactly is it that you do, Rob?" I asked, sipping more champagne and thinking that this was the nicest champers I'd had in a while.

"I work in real estate. I'm a developer, and the company we've just merged with specializes in different kinds of household inventions, which is why we are putting our heads together."

"Ah, I see. So I gather it's profitable?"

"Very." He laughed. "I wouldn't do it otherwise. It was a dream at first, but if a dream doesn't succeed after a lot of hard work, you can soon wake up from it."

"True, yes. I've had dreams like that before."

Just as I finished that sentence, the car pulled up outside one of the best restaurants in town. It was very high profile, and I'd eaten here on a couple of occasions before. It was the kind of place that didn't let just anyone in and served the most amazing food, so Rob had chosen well.

"Let's go." He smiled, as he held his hand out to me to help me out of the limousine.

Linking his arm, we ventured into the restaurant and were shown to our table. We were seated in a private booth, and the waiting staff here knew him by name, so I knew he was doing very well just through that. We were served our wine, and clinked our glasses together before we took the first sip. Sitting back and enjoying the ambience, we started to peruse the menu and talk to each other.

"So, Eleanor, tell me about yourself," Rob stated, looking up from his menu.

"What do you want to know?" I wondered, not really knowing what to divulge first - if anything, really.

"Anything to get to know you. Background, family, and then we can talk business later... or not at all." He winked.

I lay the menu on the table for a moment. "Hmm... where to begin," I thought out loud.

"There's that much, is there?" He chuckled.

"You could say that. I think after the age of thirty, everyone comes with their own variation of baggage." I smiled.

"Ah yes, we all have that. Okay, well we'll start with me, then, if you like. Ask me anything," he offered.

"Okay..." I pondered for a moment. "Have you ever been married? Do you have any children?"

"Yes, and yes. I have an ex-wife whom I was married to for three years. We drifted apart, but she's a good woman who I trust to look after our daughter... otherwise I would have custody." He laughed.

I laughed back. "Fair enough. So what else about your past should I know?"

"Erm... well, I went from rags to riches. I grew up in a poor neighborhood, and made my millions in my early twenties when I went into property development. It escalated from there, up to this stage, and it's still growing. I suppose you could say that I am blessed," he explained.

"That's actually nice. So what about you, then... any skeletons in your closet?" I chuckled.

"No, just mainly suits and some casual clothing." He chuckled. "I believe in treating everyone with the same level of respect I would expect. I don't look down on anyone with less than me in life... I think we are all trying our best. Other than that, I'm grouchy when I'm hungry." He smiled.

"We better get ordering." I laughed, perusing the menu some more.

The waiter came over and promptly took our order and the menus from us, as we sat and chatted some more.

"So how about you, Eleanor? You said you were separated?" Rob asked.

"Yes, I am. My husband walked out on me not long ago, and I still don't know why which has left me quite hurt. But anyway, at the moment I am looking to have fun with someone like-minded. I'll be honest, I do not want another relationship right now. I have three children as well... twins and a boy. They take up a lot of my thought space, and they come first with almost all of my decisions," I explained.

"We are on the same page. My daughter is always at the forefront of my mind. Plus, I'll be honest, I like to have fun. After being in an unhappy marriage, I'm not really up for anything too serious."

"I completely understand that. Shall we toast to fun, then?" I smiled, raising my glass.

"I'll drink to that." Rob smiled, clinking glasses with me and then taking a gulp.

We were served our food as we chatted some more about our everyday lives and home-life, and it was lovely to be around such a nice gentleman for the night. He was good looking and fun, and I could see why he was friends with Brandon. Rob had the same air about him - it was definitely a case of like attracts like, and they both had the same wicked sense of humor.

Later that night, being the perfect gentleman he was, Rob dropped me safely back home and wished me a good night. I'd had good food, with excellent company, and I felt wonderfully relaxed. As I stepped into the doorway, he drove away and I waved goodbye to him. He had told me that he would be calling me tomorrow to arrange another date, and I was already looking forward to it. I felt like I had my confidence back, the spring in my step, and it was now a case of onwards and upwards.

Stepping into the house, in my usual routine, I took my high heels off and placed them in the hallway. I could feel my feet relax as they were finally allowed to be placed flat on the floor and not virtually stood on my tiptoes. I tossed my purse to one side and wandered into the kitchen to get myself a glass of water. I definitely needed to ease up on all the alcohol I had been drinking lately, and wanted to chill and hydrate for the rest of the night.

A pin drop could've been heard in the house, as I tipped out the rest of my water from the glass, and then decided to go and watch a little TV before bed. It was only ten-thirty, and even though I had work the next day, I wanted to relish in the relaxed feel of the night for a bit longer.

Tossing my hair over one shoulder, I opened the door of the living room and nearly fell over in shock at witnessing none other than David, naked and spread-eagled on the sofa, with nothing more than rose petals covering his mid-region.

"What the hell are you doing?" I shouted in a lowish kind of tone, to prevent waking Natalie or the children.

"Surprise!" David grinned. "I thought you may need a little something tonight to wind down to."

"Jesus, David, anyone could have walked in here!" I gasped through the grin that was escaping my lips.

"I pretty much know the routine in this house, El. If I would've gotten caught, I would've played dumb." He chuckled.

"Played dumb?" I curiously asked.

"Yeah, if it would've been your nanny, I would've pretended to have been waiting for her. You never know, she might have taken me up on the offer." He winked.

"That's not funny, David. Anyway, how did you even get in?"

"I found a key from when me and Tasha unexpectedly started living with you a few years ago. It's not rocket science." He got up off the sofa, with the rose petals sprinkling to the ground as he stood up. He seductively walked over to me. "So…" He grinned as he gently wrapped his arms round my waist. "You know you want me…"

At this point, I didn't know whether to be amused or miffed. I'd had a date tonight, and it was a good job that I hadn't invited him in.

"David, you can't just invite yourself in whenever you want. Anyone could've walked in here tonight. I had a date, and what if I would've asked him in for coffee?" I spoke, feeling the pull of lust.

David slightly pulled away and eyed at me. "You had a date?"

"Yes, with a lovely guy who I'm glad didn't see you butt naked on my sofa!" I chuckled.

"I didn't realize you were dating now," David half-sulked.

I sighed, releasing myself from his arms and going to sit down.

"David, you knew I wasn't after anything serious with this… it's a need and a feed. We're both getting what we want, but yeah, I've been on a date tonight. As far as I'm concerned, I'm a free agent."

He came and sat next to me, and it was hard to know where to look with him being in the buff.

"I know you said that you wanted things to be light here, but I didn't think you'd be dating other men as well. Are you sleeping with him?"

I frowned at him. "Not that it's any of your business, but no, I'm not sleeping with anyone else. For goodness sake, you are on about morals, but you are sleeping with someone who is essentially a married woman. Not only that, but I'm still married to someone who is probably your arch-enemy!"

"I know. That part's kind of cool." He smiled like a little kid who was going against the rules.

I rolled my eyes. "It's not a game! To be honest, I'm now doubting my own judgement on this whole scenario."

"What? You don't think this is a good idea now?" he asked, all wide-eyed and with the whole puppy dog look that I could never master, written on his face.

"I don't know." I sighed.

"Oh, El..." He turned to me and took my hands in his. "Forget I said anything about that date guy thing... don't cut this short. I wouldn't mind having a bit more fun." He winked.

I looked at him, all bronzed, toned, and gorgeous, and even though my rational brain was screaming out at what I was doing, my libido was stepping in and shutting it up. Reaching over, I stroked my hand down his face, stopping at his jawline and leaning forward. David didn't hesitate and pulled me towards him, as the heat grew between us both.

Was this madness? Probably.

Was I going to stop it? No way.

Chapter Nine - Having a Ball

O ver the past week or so, I had been inundated with male attention, and I could see why women sometimes did this - it was really fun. I'd always known about richer women having a handful of male suitors, and I'd never thought that was something that I would ever do. Never say never! If Stephen wouldn't have walked out on me, I don't think anything like this would ever have crossed my mind, but since his unexpected departure that did leave me hurt and confused, it was a great way of regaining some of my self-esteem.

Rob had taken me on a few more dates, and we had been horseback riding, ice skating, and wine tasting. The wine tasting I hadn't minded whatsoever, and it was quite interesting, but when I told him that I wanted to have some fun, he had definitely taken that in a literal sense.

For someone who could barely balance in high heels, I wasn't too bad at horseback riding. I'd had a few lessons as a kid, but the ice skating was hilarious. Rob seemed to be somewhat of a pro, but being as pro as he was, I think I cramped his style, as he spent most of the evening trying to keep me in the upright position. He was really good fun, and I liked him a lot.

There was an easy air with him, and he was someone who, no matter what, I could've easily remained good friends with. The matter of business between our companies seemed to have been avoided, but I was sure that he would let me know at some point if he needed Rose Designs. It seemed to have faded into the background, between showering me with bouquets of flowers and kisses, and he was completely wonderful.

I'd had a few more 'sessions' with David, too, which was another thing that I was enjoying. I felt like a woman when he was with me - not a mother, a wife, a businesswoman - but just a woman, and that made me feel alive. It was kind of a thrill knowing that he had wanted me since day one, and I was finally letting him have his cake and eat it. I didn't want anything else from him, and a part of me still wondered why the hell I'd gone anywhere near David, but I was at a point where I couldn't care less. I was thirty - well, a couple of years older, but let's not go there - flirty, and having the time of my life.

Anyhow, tonight was the night, and I couldn't wait! Everything had been prepped and organized for the grand ball in honor of the expansion of Rose Designs, and I had been running around like a twit for the past week due to it. Clarisse had, of course, been amazing with the organization, and that was something that I definitely hadn't inherited. I was scatter-brained at the best of times, so having the back-up of someone who was super-organized was always a winner.

The venue was set, and I'd had professional party planners in to sort out what the hotel looked like, and to make sure that the staff there were meeting the demands. The finest in society were invited, and it was set to be one of the biggest events that had happened in a while. We could sense the media buzz around it, which to be fair I wasn't really used to; but all publicity for the expansion was more than welcome.

I'd also been in near-constant contact with Caroline as well, and she had sorted the staffing out, for what would be the department store on the ground floor of the building. Everything was falling into place, and considering I had not long separated from my husband, I was feeling pretty darn good and I wanted it to stay that way.

Caroline had arranged the invites, as she was the one with a list as long as my arm (if not much longer), of the best business contacts that should be there. She'd also told me that she was going to be escorted to the venue by a handsome man named Geoffrey, as apparently it was always good for a lady to have a handsome man to escort her to these types of events. I couldn't really understand it, but I could see why it probably would look good for the cameras.

Deciding that I wasn't really comfortable with asking anyone else to accompany me, the first person I thought of was David. He had the looks and was photogenic, and he was also going to be working for me. I wasn't about to tag along with someone who had no connections whatsoever to the business, just to 'look good'. He was the perfect candidate. I'd called him up and asked him whether he would be my escort for the evening, and I could tell by the tone of his voice that he was slightly thrilled at being asked. I hoped that he didn't read too much into it, but I didn't have time to worry about that.

Everyone from Rose Designs was due to be there, including Caroline's contacts, and of course people like Jeanie and Tasha - the people who'd had a hand in making Rose Designs what it was today. All-in-all we were set to have about four-hundred guests at the venue, and I gulped at the thought of having to be hostess for that many people. But there would be a band playing and free food and drink, so I suppose that that was probably what most people would be going for anyway.

So with half an hour to spare, I checked myself over in the mirror. I'd had Roger do my hair and makeup, and was wearing a black, glitzy gown which I'd had custom made. I was ready to go and felt like a princess, which is exactly what I had wanted. This was a landmark moment, which highlighted how far I'd come since building the business up from the ground.

As I gave myself a glance over, I thought about my father and wished he could've been here. My heart ached for his presence, and I knew how proud he would have been. Taking a deep breath and fighting back the lump in my throat, I patted my dress down to make sure that I looked just so.

"Miss. Eleanor! Your car is here!" Penny shouted up the stairs to me.

Excitedly, I gripped the bottom of my dress to make sure that I wasn't going to be falling over, and made my way as hastily as I could down the stairs. At the bottom of the staircase, Penny, Roger, Natalie, and the children, were stood waiting, and all looking my way to probably admire my dress and wish me a goodbye.

"Mommy, you look beautiful!" Mason called out, with his little face peeping up at me as I walked over to them all.

"Aw, thank you, my little soldier. Mommy loves you and I'll see you in the morning." I leant down and gave him a kiss on the forehead. Then in turn, I did the same for Madison and Henry.

I loved these children with all my heart, and I loved the fact that I was holding this ball because of the business doing so well, and that business would be theirs one day.

Standing upright, Roger was the next to approach me. "Chica, you look bellisimo," he whispered, eyes watering.

"It's all thanks to you, Roger." I blushed, while he leant forward and gave me a light hug as to not smudge my makeup.

"You have a wonderful night, Miss. Eleanor." Penny smiled, doing the same as Roger.

"I will. Thanks, all. I will see you in the morning. Love you."

They all said goodbye to me as I walked outside. Looking down the steps, the limousine was there, with David holding the door open for me. I didn't know what it was, but a hint of sadness hit me when I saw him. For the past however many years, it had always been Stephen at the car door, but tonight it was not meant to be. I had to snap out of that thought-train, though, so I took another deep breath, smiled, and walked toward the car.

"You look stunning, El," David spoke, his eyes lighting up upon seeing me.

"Thank you. You look very handsome," I replied.

"I aim to please." He winked, as I gracefully slid into the car and he closed the door behind me.

David got into the other side and we set off for the hotel. I quickly checked my cell for any updates about anything, but there was just a text from Clarisse, saying that she couldn't wait to see me there. I was looking forward to seeing her, too, and apart from the other few hundred revelers that were invited, I was looking forward to spending some time with those nearest and dearest to me.

Pulling up outside of the hotel, the venue was buzzing with paparazzi at the entrance. There was a length of red carpet lay out from the entrance up to where the cars were stopping, with barriers along each side to keep the media at bay. Further up ahead, some of our more prestigious guests were emerging from their cars, and the camera flashes were going nuts. I gulped at the sight of it. I wasn't used to being the centre of attention like this, but I knew I had to get over the whole stage-fright thing if I wanted to make the business a success.

The car pulled over, and the chauffeur whipped around to the passenger side to let us both out. David got out first and then reached back in to take my hand. Stepping out of the car in my black gown, I was glad I had made the effort tonight. I knew that there was going to be media here, but I didn't expect the extent of it to look like this.

The cameras flashed in our direction, as I linked David's arm, and he smiled towards the photographers. I wasn't sure that I looked so much like a starlet, but more like a rabbit caught in headlights. Letting David lead the way, we stopped halfway up the red carpet to pose for a few shots.

In the midst of the media buzz, I could hear a few shouts from the paparazzi:

"Mrs. Rose, how are the plans for the department store coming along?"

"Is it true that you are going to have the Governor open the new premises?"

"Will your products be appealing to the more upmarket clientele?" came the shouts, as I stood there, with David leaning over to me, whispering in my ear to smile, nod, and not say anything.

I was glad David was with me, as throughout his modeling career, he had probably become accustomed to these scenarios way more than I had ever been. I probably would have stopped outside for a good half an hour trying to answer their questions.

Then the final cry of, *"Where is your husband tonight, Mrs. Rose?"* came bellowing out of one journalists mouth, and I knew it was time to go inside.

Feeling foolish after hearing that question, it slightly took the buzz off being here. As David led me inside by my arm and we wandered into the grand venue, I couldn't help but feel hypocritical. I had built the whole business on the basis of my love for my husband, and yet, where was he tonight? He was probably shacked up with some other woman, and I was attending this event with the guy I had been sleeping with. I had to pull it together - whatever basis this company was built on, this was an important night and needed to be dealt with.

Entering the grand venue which was situated in a large ballroom next to the gardens of the hotel, the place was alive with the chatter of guests and the sound of music emanating from the DJ on stage. Everyone was dressed in their black and white finery, and it was a vision in itself.

As we were served some champagne from one of the waiting staff, Clarisse was the first one to approach us. Giving David a quick, stern side-glance, she pulled me into a hug to say hello.

"Hi, sweetheart!" she beamed. "It's all going swimmingly. Were you okay with the paps outside?" she asked thoughtfully.

"Yes, I was fine, thanks. Aw, I'm so pleased it's going so well. I always have the feeling that I'll arrive and nobody is here." I chuckled.

Clarisse smiled. "Not tonight. This is turning out to be a huge success! You should give yourself a pat on the back. Anyway, I'm off to schmooze some more." She winked, as she started to walk away.

"Mom!" I shouted to her, as she turned back around to face me. "Thanks so much for your help from day one." I smiled warmly. "Will you come up onstage with me later, to make my speech?" I asked, like a little child that didn't want to be left on their own.

"Of course." She smiled back, before turning away and making her way back into the bustle of guests.

"So, where do you need me to escort you next?" David asked, placing his hand on mine that was linking his arm.

I sighed. "Home?" I joked.

David laughed. "This is your night! You can't go home! Come on, let's float about the room, and you stop wherever you want to."

Agreeing with that plan, we made our way into the crowd. I wasn't sure about stopping where I wanted to - I had to greet each and every one of the guests that were present. I had personally invited a lot of them, and we stopped in conversation a few times. I introduced David as my new store manager to a few people there, as they were looking at him a bit strangely and no doubt wondering why he was on my arm. Once they had a brief explanation that he would soon be a comrade in arms, their look changed from one of bewilderment, to appreciatively nodding at who he actually was.

As we walked on, I was met by the smiling face of one of my most prestigious guests, Beau Blakemore. He was a billionaire from Texas, and we had catered for his wife's business a few years ago.

"Eleanor Rose." He smiled, as he made his way forward and shook my hand.

"Beau Blakemore, it's good to see you again." I smiled back.

"Eleanor, if I may introduce you to my wife, Kate." He grinned proudly, edging her forward from his arm.

"I'm very pleased to meet you, Eleanor." Kate smiled, also shaking my hand.

"It's a pleasure, Kate." I smiled back at her, turning to David. "Kate, Beau, this is a close friend of mine, and my soon-to-be manager, David." They politely shook hands and greeted each other, while I turned back to Kate. "So tell me, how is your floristry business going?"

"Wonderful, thanks to yourselves. Business is booming and I'm so happy," she replied, with her plush English accent coming through - I could've listened to that all night.

"Brilliant. I hope you both enjoy your night. It's been so good to finally meet you, Kate, and great to see you again, Beau." I smiled.

"It's always a pleasure to see you. We'll talk business again soon." He tipped the Stetson he was wearing, took Kate's hand, and walked away.

David leant into me. "Who was that?" He grinned.

"Beau and Kate Blakemore. He owns an oil company and is one of the richest men on the planet. They have been very good customers. They are a lovely couple as well," I explained.

"Ah, I see." He nodded, taking my arm as we moved on. "I might invest in one of those Stetson's... it looked good on him."

I chuckled. "I think it fits in with him being a Texan, David. You just stick with your own style."

David laughed and took my arm again. Merging onwards, I hadn't even managed to drink the glass of champagne I had been given, because I was too busy in conversation, but next we bumped into Caroline.

"Eleanor, darling! What a success this is!" she beamed my way, bringing me into a light hug.

"Yes, it is," I agreed. "It's all going really well. Thank you so much for all your help with this."

"My pleasure." She turned her attention to David. "I hope you are on your best behavior tonight." She smirked toward him.

"Of course," David politely replied. "I'm here to support Eleanor." He smiled toward me.

"Good to hear," she replied in a stern manner toward him. "Anyway," she continued, turning back toward me, "I will have to continue my way around all of these people. I look forward to your speech later. Enjoy the night!" she beamed.

"I will, thank you, Caroline. Enjoy the night, too."

We parted ways, until eventually we saw Tasha in a group of people, with Jenson standing near to her, whom she had modeled with on my range before. I unhooked my arm from David, as we drew nearer to her - I did not want to be drawing the wrong attention from her tonight. I couldn't be bothered with any funny looks, tantrums, or questions from her at this event.

"Eleanor!" she cried out as we got nearer to her.

"Hi, Tash. You look lovely tonight!" I smiled.

"Great party!" she replied, then looked at David stood behind me. "I didn't expect you to be here."

"He's going to be the new store manager, so anyone associated with the business is going to be here tonight," I replied.

"Oh yeah! Sorry, I forgot about that!" Tasha beamed while snorting, with her immaturity smiling through. "Aw, it's nice that you two are getting along again. One big happy family, eh?"

"Yeah...." I cautiously replied, noting David breaking into a grin next to me. "Anyway, Tash, enjoy yourself, and I'll have to go and make my speech soon. Is your mom here?"

"Yeah, she's around somewhere in the crowd." Tasha giggled, scanning around her. "Good luck with your speech!"

Tasha turned her attention back to Jenson and the others she was with, and I was glad that part was over and done with. Walking further away from her, David was by my side again as we moved about the room.

"One big happy family, eh?" he joked next to me.

"I couldn't believe she said that." I chuckled. "More like one big dysfunctional family."

David leant into me. "There's nothing dysfunctional about what we have been getting up to." He smirked.

I shot him a look of horror. "Er, not the time, David. Remember, this is a professional event?"

"Of course." He winked, as he stood upright again and scanned the room.

"I'll have to do my speech now before any food gets served," I stated, noting how the doors to the venue had been closed, meaning that everyone who had been invited had arrived.

"Your stage awaits." David grinned. "Do you want me to go up with you?"

"No, I'll be fine. You stay here. I've got to find Clarisse."

Leaving David standing alone, I felt a bit sorry for him. Nowadays he was a bit out of his depth around these people, as I'm sure a fair few knew about his dealings with Radar. But, with his gift of the gab, I was sure that he would be absolutely fine.

Milling through the sea of people who were greeting me and saying what a great party it was, as I waded through, I finally caught a glimpse of Clarisse talking to one of our clients. Walking up to them, I politely interrupted.

"Sorry, can I steal Clarisse away for a moment?" I smiled sweetly.

The group of guests raised their glasses in approval, and I gently took Clarisse's arm, as she knew the drill that I wanted to get the speech done and out of the way.

"Ready, Eleanor?" She smiled, as she held my hand in front of the stage.

"As I'll ever be. My knees are like jelly." I chuckled.

"You'll be fine once you get into it. Good luck." She grinned, ushering me onto the stage.

Taking one step at a time, I graced the stage, and prompted the DJ to stop playing for a moment. He handed me the microphone, and as the music died down, so did the chatter. I nervously looked on at the huge crowd before me - it was definitely the biggest crowd I'd ever had to talk in front of in my entire life.

Taking a deep breath, I began:

"Good evening, ladies and gentlemen, and thank you all for attending this event in honor of the Rose Designs expansion."

At those words, the crowd cheered and clapped, and it was nice that it hadn't fallen on deaf ears. I suddenly thought back to when I was invited to the Radar expansion, and how the little bald man was stood on the stage talking, and I had completely ignored what he was saying thanks to Bryant.

"I would just like to thank you all, as if it wasn't for each and every part that you all have played, we would not be where we are today. There are that many people that I am sincerely thankful for, it would be impossible for me to mention all names, but I am touched by their loyalty, love, and guidance, and I would like them to know that they always have my support. On that note, I would just like to bring my second-in-command further onto the stage...'

Turning to Clarisse, I ushered her toward me. In her surprise, she slowly stepped forward - I don't think she was expecting me to put her in the spotlight for this speech.

"Clarisse is not only a business partner, but she is family, and I owe her so much respect. This lady works so hard, and I could've never have asked for a more important and wonderful lady to grace both my business world, and personal world.'

A round of applause erupted in the audience.

"Now, without further ado, if you would do me the honor of raising your glasses... to Rose Designs! May she bloom, flourish, and grace the business world with her beauty!"

Raising my glass, the audience followed suit, as they all repeated "Rose Designs" at the top of their lungs. When everyone had taken a sip of their drink, there was another round of applause and whooping noises coming from the hundreds of guests, as I turned to Clarisse, took her hand, smiled, and walked off the stage with her.

"Thank you so much, Eleanor. That was a beautiful speech, and I was not expecting it," Clarisse voiced to me as we reached the bottom step with tears filling her eyes.

"I spoke nothing but the truth. You deserve so much praise. I love you, Mom." I warmly smiled.

"I love you too," Clarisse whispered back, bringing me into another hug as I could feel the warmth emanate from her.

Breaking the hug, we both composed ourselves and ventured back into the crowd. Clarisse went off one way, while business contacts and employees alike were stopping me and saying what a great speech that was. I was thrilled that not only was it over with, but that I'd done a lot of that speech off the top of my head and it had gone down so well.

The music ramped up again and food was served, as the night went from good to great. The atmosphere was lovely, and I was overjoyed that things were turning out as planned - and actually better than I ever could have imagined. I got to meet future employees that Caroline was introducing me to, and also potential future investors. The future was looking brighter by the moment, and I wasn't just talking about the spotlights from the stage area that were dazzling my eyes.

As I was talking to some employees that worked for me, and were asking about different parts of the business expansion, in the corner of my eye I noticed a familiar face venturing over - Rob. I made my excuses to the people I was talking to and turned to him, giving him a big smile to welcome him.

"Rob! Lovely to see you!" I smiled as I gave him a hug.

"It's good to be here! I was looking for Brandon. Have you seen him yet?" he asked.

"No, not yet. There's that many people here, I haven't had chance to get around everyone. I will do soon. Anyway, it's lovely to see you here. I didn't know whether you would come or not. I know I mentioned it when I last saw you."

"I wouldn't have missed it for the world. It's a great night. I must admit, this has outdone my party." He chuckled.

"It hasn't." I laughed. "It's just different tastes... plus party planners had a major hand in this. I can't take credit for all of it."

"Party planners had a hand in mine, but I'll have to get the number of the ones you used." He grinned. "Anyway, I was wondering, and I know you are busy, but I was wondering if I could have a private word with you?"

"Now?" I wondered.

"If possible. I could catch up with you later, but the sooner I get this off my chest, the better." He chuckled.

Intrigued, I agreed, and we made our way to the back of the venue to where the gardens were. Exiting the grand French doors at the back, it was actually nice to get out of the heat of the room for a moment. The gardens were beautifully decorated with all different flower arrangements, and with solar lights dazzling with all different colors, it was magical outside. A few other people were in the gardens as well, obviously for a breath of fresh air, but it was fairly quiet and was a better place for a private conversation.

"What was it you wanted to talk to me about?" I asked, turning to him.

Rob looked awkward as he shifted on the spot. "Well, I, erm... you know what, I am so much better at business dealings than personal ones." He chuckled.

I narrowed my eyes at him. "Is everything okay?"

He looked at me. "No, well, yes... but I would like it to be better."

I sighed. 'Listen, if you didn't want to see me again, that's fine. Usually men don't call, but if you've had second thoughts about another date, then you don't need to explain yourself to me," I soothed.

Rob chuckled, his bright blue eyes glinting from the nearby lights that were shimmering away in the backdrop. "No, I think you've misread the situation."

"That does sound like me." I chuckled back. "So what is it you wanted to talk to me about?"

Rob sighed, looking down at the floor and then back up at me again, taking my hand in his.

"I wanted to talk, to firstly thank you for the wonderful dates that we have been on. The ice skating in particular was amusing." He grinned, as I, of course, blushed at the memory of falling into his arms over and over again. "I know that you said you didn't want anything serious, and at first I was totally inclined to agree." He paused and I felt my stomach flip - I had a good idea what was coming next. "I really like you, Eleanor, and I think we could have something special. I don't usually move so fast, unless it's closing a business deal, but with you, it feels so right."

Standing there speechless, a part of me was mentally kicking myself for dating him. I knew that this would happen, and I'd even said to David that if I got involved with someone else, there'd be a chance that they would want something more. Yet I'd gone against my better judgment, due to the fact that I thought Rob wanted to date and be more carefree about things.

I looked at his hand that was holding mine. I really liked him, but I didn't know what to say.

"Erm..." I mumbled awkwardly in reply.

"I know it's quick. I've been wondering myself if it was the right thing to do, and I understand if you want to think more about things. It's just, I would like you by my side." He paused again, tightening his grasp around mine. "I think I love you."

I nearly fell over. We'd gone from dating, to he liked me, and now he loved me? My mind was all over the place - I barely knew what day it was most of the time, and I'd never thought things with him would become this serious, so soon.

"Oh, er, Rob..." I muttered.

"I know, I've put you on the spot, and this is your night, so I do apologize for landing this on you now. I had to let you know what my feelings were before I completely bottled it." He shyly smiled. "I'll let you think on it. Is it okay if I call you tomorrow?" he asked.

"Er, yes," I answered, not knowing where to put myself.

Rob leant forward and placed a soft kiss on my lips.

What was I doing? I'd originally set out to have some fun, but now that feelings were involved, it was creating more of a mess than anything. I savored his kiss - he was rich, smart, and incredibly handsome, so I may as well enjoy one part of the encounter.

He pulled away, lightly squeezing my hand and then letting go, heading back into the venue and leaving me standing outside, dumbfounded at what had been said. As I stood there in thought, a voice broke into my bubble.

"Hey, there you are." It was David coming striding into the gardens.

"Oh, hey." I looked up at him, still in a world of my own.

"I've been looking for you. I brought you a drink." He smiled, handing me a glass of champagne.

"Thanks," I replied, still feeling distant.

"Everything okay? You look a little pale." David eyed me in concern.

"Yes, I'm fine." I smiled, snapping out of it and lying through my teeth, staring at mess-number-two who had just handed me a drink. "I came out for some air."

"I was just dancing with Tash. She was saying that she wants me to have Reece tomorrow night, because she's going out with Jenson," he explained.

"Oh. Right. That's nice, isn't it? How do you feel about that?" I wondered, eyeing David for a reaction of the mother of his child dating Jenson, whilst he babysat.

"Fine." He shrugged. "She can do what she likes. I have my sights set in a more pleasing direction." He grinned my way.

Great - someone else who was probably after more than a quick fling in my pool house. David opened his arm up for me to link again, and I took it as we headed back inside. Rob had disappeared from view and back into the crowd, and I was glad that it was so busy. I couldn't be doing with bumping into him again, and him probably looking at me and wondering what I would actually say in reply to his declaration of love.

Looking around, I hadn't seen sight nor sound of Brandon, and I wouldn't have minded talking to him about this. He was both friends with me and Rob, so perhaps he could've given me some guidance of letting Rob down gently - if I chose to do so. I didn't know what to think. I had been so fixated on tonight and making it a success, that I really didn't have any head-space for anything else.

As the night wore on, the music slowed to a light melody, as a few of the guests were starting to depart. They said their goodbyes to me, and eventually I saw Brandon, who made his way over.

"I was beginning to think you were a figment of my imagination." I chuckled, as he strode over, and I was propping up the bar on my own.

Brandon laughed. "I looked for you before, but I couldn't see you. I thought I would quickly say a hello and goodbye, as to not be rude." He winked.

"Ah, you could never be rude." I smiled. "So how did you find tonight?"

"Good, yeah. You throw a good party. I was talking to quite a few of my own business contacts that were here. Plus it was quite a bash... I usually only come for the free food and drink." He grinned.

"Of course." I smiled. "Did you speak to Rob, tonight?" I eyed, not giving any details away.

"Hmm, yeah I did," Brandon replied, sipping the rest of his drink.

Just as he was about to continue, Caroline wandered over to me.

"Sorry to interrupt," she spoke, as myself and Brandon turned our attention to her, "but I must be going now. I've had enough champagne for one night." She laughed.

"Aw, that's no worries. Thanks so much for everything. I think most people are leaving now," I replied.

"Yes, I see quite a few people are heading for their cars as we speak. I'll see you on Monday when the new premises open."

That was another thing I gulped at - it was Friday now, and was a mere three days until the grand opening of the new building. I could have done with an extra week to make sure everything was prepared, but time was money, and I knew the sooner we opened, the better.

"You sure will. I will see you first thing Monday," I replied.

"Indeed. Goodnight, Eleanor." Caroline gave me a light hug, before her security joined her once again, along with whom I could only assume was her date for the evening, and they left to go home.

I turned back to Brandon. "Sorry, where were we?"

"Rob," Brandon stated.

At those words, something, or someone caught my eye over Brandon's shoulder. At first, my eyes couldn't focus on what I was seeing, but soon came into view. I blinked hard, as Brandon was saying something to me, but not a word of it was going in. I shook my head - I thought I was seeing things - but there, in the background, was Stephen.

"Eleanor, Eleanor... are you okay?" Brandon's voice came back into earshot.

Gawking at Brandon, wide-eyed, I then looked back over his shoulder, at Stephen who was clearly stood in my eyeline. Standing up from leaning on the bar, I looked at him. Even with all the guests milling around, I could clearly see my estranged husband, standing there in the middle of the function room, looking straight at me.

"Stephen," I whispered in shock.

"What? Where?" Brandon asked, looking around him.

Just as it looked like Stephen was about to take a step toward me, I recoiled as a lady drew near to him; a lady in a black dress, and one that I knew all too well - Darcy. As I watched on, she took his arm and started pulling him away from approaching me.

What the hell was she doing here, or with him?! I watched as Stephen sheepishly put his head down, and seemed to, although reluctantly, walk away and follow her, eyeing me from over his shoulder, with a long, pleading look filling his eyes.

"Stephen!" I called out, wanting to know what the hell was going on.

My mind whirled, as Brandon asked me once again where he was, but I was too distracted. I faintly saw him disappear out of view, and get lost in the crowd that was milling out of the doors.

"I have to talk to him," I hastily announced, as I shot toward the doors, with Brandon following me on behind.

"Eleanor! You can't leave... you've still got guests here!" Brandon called after me. "Where's he gone?"

As I reached the doors, he had disappeared from view, and other guests who were either in the room or waiting for their cars were looking at me strangely. I had to pull it together, to get through tonight. His random appearance could not affect what was occurring around me.

I turned to Brandon. "Stephen was here, but he wasn't alone," I stated, feeling the lump of upset in my throat.

"Why, who was he with?" Brandon asked, looking at me concerned.

"Darcy," I replied, unable to believe the name I was uttering out of my own mouth.

"What? That friend who ditched you at the bar?" he recalled.

"Yes, that one. But she wasn't invited. I just don't understand what's going on. It looked like he wanted to talk to me."

"Yes, but do you want to talk to him?" Brandon queried.

"Yes. No. I don't know…" I muttered, feeling confused at the wave of emotion running through my veins.

"Come on, let's get you a drink, of something preferably non-alcoholic." He kindly smiled, as he took my arm and led me to the bar.

Leaning over the counter, he asked the bartender for a pot of tea, and even though the bartender looked confused at the odd request, he obliged.

Sipping on my tea, I had a few interruptions by more guests who were leaving, but I was glad it was the end of the night. I would have happily turned everyone out of the building when I saw Stephen, but while a part of me would have wanted to speak to him - mainly for an explanation of his behavior - another part of me hated how he had treated me.

When the room was near-empty, with only a few small groups left, I was glad to have some breathing space. Brandon sat with me and kept me company, as he tried to take my mind off things and keep me focused on getting through the night, and I was relieved for his support.

As the last of the guests milled out of the venue, Jeanie emerged from somewhere in the room that I wasn't focused on, and made her way over.

"Eleanor," she began with some urgency, "I didn't want to disturb you before, but did you see Stephen tonight?"

"Yes, I did. Did you invite him?" I wondered.

"No. I briefly saw him before. He gave me a strange sort of smile, but then he looked like he was looking for someone… which I can only presume was you," she explained.

"I saw him before, but he wasn't alone," I stated.

"Who was he with?" she asked.

"Darcy," came my unimpressed reply.

Jeanie shook her head in the same manner I had done earlier on. "What? Darcy, David's sister?" she replied, barely able to believe her own ears.

I nodded. "Yes, her. He was looking at me, and then as he was about to come over, she pulled him away. I didn't even invite her, and I don't know what the hell she was doing with him! Have you met Darcy yet?" I wondered.

"No. Whenever her and Tasha have got together, she picks her up at the end of the drive, or meets her somewhere," Jeanie replied.

"Where's Tasha now?" I asked, scanning the near-empty room.

"She left before with Jenson." She sighed. "I doubt she knows anything, as she would have definitely told me if Darcy would have mentioned Stephen."

I sighed and placed my head in my hands. "I don't believe this tonight."

Brandon placed his arm around my shoulders. "Do you want me to take you home?" he offered.

I raised my head. "I was here with David. I'm supposed to be going home in the car with him." I looked around. "I can't see him."

Just as I uttered the words, David came through the front doors and was striding his way over to us.

"What's wrong?" he asked over to me, as I was sat surrounded by Jeanie and Brandon.

"It's been a long night," I replied to him.

"By the way, Jeanie, Brandon, Brandon, Jeanie," I introduced, realizing that I'd forgotten my manners in the middle of the mess.

"It's okay, me and Brandon have briefly met before, when he came to look around Rose Designs," she recalled.

"Oh yeah, sorry," I mumbled.

"I gather you are Stephen's mom, and Eleanor's mother-in-law?" Brandon politely asked.

"Yes, I am. Although I could wring the neck of my son right now," she stated in an agitated tone.

"Listen, Jeanie, it's not your fault how he is behaving. I don't think any of us know what he's doing," I replied, trying to soothe her of any guilt.

"What are you guys talking about?" David asked as he reached us.

Jeanie and Brandon looked at me, not knowing whether I was going to impart any information onto David. Little did either of them know what was going on between me and him at the moment.

"Stephen was here," I voiced to David.

"You're joking me!" David exclaimed, looking around him. "What did he want?"

Jeanie narrowed her eyes at David, as I subtly told him through my facial expressions not to be giving anything away.

"He left before we could talk," I explained.

"What, why? Was he alone?" David asked.

I looked at Jeanie first, and could see the look on her face, as I turned back to David.

"He was with your sister," I bluntly replied.

His face crumpled into confusion. "My sister?" he practically squeaked.

"I'm gathering you don't know why," Brandon asked, cutting in.

David narrowed his eyes at Brandon. "And you are?" he bluntly asked.

"Oh, Brandon, this is my ex-husband, David. David, this is Brandon... a business associate, and friend," I quickly introduced.

Brandon shook hands with David, with the whole tug of war of handshake occurring. After a moment, they both let go.

"You've been married more than once?" Brandon queried, looking amused.

"Yes," I grinned, "but that's a conversation for another day."

Brandon nodded in agreement, as we all turned back to the matter at hand.

"I'm going to get going, then, Eleanor," Jeanie spoke.

"Oh yes, of course. Are you okay getting home?" I wondered.

"I'll call a cab." She smiled.

"No need. I will happily give you a ride home," Brandon offered.

"Aw, that's very kind of you. Thank you, Brandon." Jeanie smiled.

"I'll call on you tomorrow, Eleanor," Brandon stated. "Goodnight, and thank you for yet another interesting night." He smirked.

"Goodnight." I chuckled, as he took Jeanie's arm and they headed out of the door.

"Are you ready to go?" David asked, holding his arm out to me.

"Yes, definitely." I sighed, linking him.

"Do you want me to stay over tonight?" he wondered.

"If I'm honest, I don't know what I want. I think it's best that you go home tonight. I need to rest and recharge. Plus if Penny sees you in the morning, I don't think she will be held responsible for her actions." I smirked.

"Fair enough." David smirked back.

We walked out into the silent night air. The buzz of chatter had died down, and all the guests had departed from the venue. Tonight had been one of the strangest nights of my life, and that in itself was pretty remarkable.

David opened the car door for me and I got inside. As I sat back in the seat and we headed off for my house, I took in the scenery. There were people in the distance, walking along together and seemingly having a normal existence. I thought I'd achieved that existence when I had found Stephen, but I guess it was a fallacy.

Laying my head back on the seat, I thought about Rob's revelations, and the fact that David was always edging for more than a quick hook up every now and then. I wasn't sure what was in my perfume, but it seemed to be addictive, and I chuckled to myself when I thought that maybe I would have to try a new brand.

Entering a little world of my own - any world was better than stark reality - I wondered what the next day would bring. Rob had said he was going to call me, and I had no idea what to tell him. Brandon told me he was going to call around, and I didn't want my friendship with him to be affected if I turned his friend down. I guess that my life was always meant to be out of the ordinary, and it didn't seem like that was going to change any time soon.

Tomorrow was indeed another day, and who knew what would happen.

Chapter Ten - Accumulation

Waking up the next morning, I felt pretty weary about the night before. It had been a roaring success in business terms, but in personal terms, it had been a bit of a disaster. I'd racked my brains all night, wondering why Stephen was there at the event, and why the hell Darcy was with him, pulling him away.

Did they know each other?

She was David's sister, but even David hadn't seen her for years. No, that definitely wasn't the connection. One thing did click, though; Stephen's behavior had changed dramatically after the night of the yacht party that Darcy had held, but I couldn't understand why. He'd never mentioned anything to me, and Darcy seemed normal that night. There was certainly more to this than met the eye.

Stephen's behavior had been so unlike him, but how much did I really know a person after five years of marriage? Some couples went through their entire lives without really knowing each other - my father and ex-fake-mother being one of them. Stephen was a strong man as well, and I'd never seen him cow-tail and follow anyone else around like that in my entire life, but maybe he did with me?

Perhaps they'd struck up an affair, or something? But the way Stephen had looked at Darcy when they'd first met, it didn't make any sense. It wasn't the look of love or lust, that's for sure.

When my mind wasn't desperately trying to come up with an adequate explanation for that dilemma, it switched to Rob. A guy that I hadn't known long at all, and had only been on a few dates with, had professed his love for me. What the hell was I going to do about that one?

Geez, Eleanor, this whole 'not mixing work with pleasure' business was really paying off - sarcasm duly noted.

Then there was David. David whom I had been previously married to. He had schemed behind my back to take Pearl Designs, he had led my sister-in-law up the garden path and then gotten her pregnant, and had had a massive co-caine habit which he had not long emerged from rehab for.

What a catch, Eleanor. What a catch.

Now, just because I'm me, I had decided that since his apparent character transplant since leaving rehab, it would be a really good idea to sleep with the guy. Geez, I think I was the one who needed a major life-choice overhaul.

Burying my head in the pillow, I thought about what a mess it all was. I suppose I always knew in the back of my mind that it would end in disaster, but that damn ego of mine had muffled it.

Now I had Rob wanting answers as to whether I would consider being more serious with him, David was always pleading with those puppy dog eyes, and I had a husband who was apparently shacking up with a so-called 'friend'.

I was a mother of three, for goodness sake! I should've just stuck with Brandon - he was gay, and that would have been a lot safer to be around with my raging hormones.

"Miss. Eleanor!" Penny shouted through the bedroom door.

"Oh, it's Saturday, Penny! I want to stay in bed!" I cried out, my voice being muffled by the pillow I was lying face-down on and smothering myself with.

"Should I tell the gentleman to go away?!" Penny shouted back.

Gentleman? What gentleman?

"Who is it, Penny?" I shouted back, raising my head from the pillow and eager to hear the response.

"A gentleman called Rob!" she shouted through.

My face creased in confusion - I checked the clock and it was 11am! Oops, I suppose I had slept in for a change. But, seriously? That wasn't really giving me much thinking space.

"Tell him I'll be down in a minute!" I shouted back. "I need to get dressed."

"Okay!" Penny shouted through, before vacating back downstairs.

I quickly dove around the bedroom, trying to grab some clean clothes and wondering if I had time for a shower. My hair was stuck up like a glowing por-cupine, and I was wondering what in the world I could do with it at such short notice, to try and look remotely presentable.

"Miss. Eleanor!" Penny shouted again, as I was trying to hook my leg into a pair of skinny jeans.

"Yes?" I replied, really frustrated with these damn spray-on jeans.

"Rob said he would be back in an hour! He's just got to go somewhere!" Penny replied.

Phew! I had time to get ready.

"Thanks, Penny!" I shouted back, relieved that I could now get a shower and look like I was a human being.

Whipping off the jeans that I was trying to place on, I bolted for the bathroom. Showering quickly, I thought about what I would say to him - and came up with nothing. I couldn't decide what to say for the best.

Was that awful? I was willing to string him along a little longer because I was stuck between complex relationships. I thought about social media and wondered whether there was a t-shirt you could wear at times like this, which had 'it's complicated' on it for all to see. That might have warded off the potential suitors, while I figured out what I did actually want.

After showering, I dried my hair off and brushed it back into a presentable ponytail, and placed on my skinny jeans and t-shirt. I wasn't in the mood to dress up in any way, shape, or form after last night, so he would have to take me as he found me.

Rushing downstairs, I was just in time to catch Natalie, heading out of the front door with the children. They were off to another group that Natalie knew of, so I gave them all big cuddles and kisses before wishing them a good day. I was glad they would be out of the house while I spoke to Rob, as this really wasn't a thing I wanted my children to be witnessing. I wasn't in the habit of introducing men to my children. Their father had upped sticks and left them, and in their little minds, that was hard enough for them to comprehend without me adding to the mix.

I wandered into the kitchen for some 'brunch', as after a night of tossing and turning I had managed to successfully drift off through breakfast, and grabbed some bacon and bagels from Penny.

"How are you this morning, Miss. Eleanor?" Penny asked as she washed a few dishes.

"Hmm, good, Penny," I replied, lost in my thoughts of how to handle Rob today.

"He's a fine gentleman, isn't he?" Penny mused in my direction.

"Yeah, he's great," I replied back, still in a world of my own at the breakfast table.

Penny placed the dishcloth down and came to join me in the next seat with a cup of tea.

"You do seem very distracted, Miss. Eleanor. Is everything okay?" she asked, caringly tilting her head to one side.

"Huh? What? Sorry, Penny. I'm completely away with it this morning," I muttered, snapping back to attention.

"I can tell." She chuckled. "Well, you know what they say... a problem shared..."

I looked at Penny and wondered whether she would really want to know what was going on in my mind. I was so lost, though, so maybe she could impart some wisdom.

'Penny," I began, straightening myself up in my chair, "have you ever been involved with more than one man at once?"

Penny looked shocked, as she practically inhaled the tea she was sipping. "What?" She chuckled. "Erm, it's put me on the spot..."

"Sorry, it's just I don't know what to do." I sighed, slumping back over in my chair and munching on a piece of bacon.

"There was one man. My... I fell for him head over heels," Penny began, as my interest was suddenly peaked and I sat upright to face her. "He was a beautiful man, but he was in de armed forces, and he went away a lot. It wasn't meant to be. He broke my heart when he married someone else, plus my parents did not approve of him... he had a rebellious streak." She grinned to herself as she was deep in thought.

"What happened then?" I wondered, willing her to go on.

"I met my late-husband. He was in a mess at de time, with being in a gang and trying to get out of it. But there was a kindness with him... a kindness like no other. I fell for that more than anything else. Yes, the first man that I loved had de strength, de looks, de charisma... but when I met my husband, I just knew. I knew that we had each other's back. We had both been hurt and we would become each other's salvation. We produced beautiful daughters together, who I would not change for the world. I look at them, and that's what makes it all worthwhile." She warmly smiled.

I sighed heavily. "You see, that's all I want, Penny. To find that one man who will be there through everything. I thought I had that with Stephen, but after recent times, my opinion of him has dramatically changed."

"Do you not love him anymore, Miss. Eleanor?"

"Yes, I do," I quietly replied. "But I also hate the way he has treated both me and the children, and after what happened in my pregnancy, and he wasn't here... I don't think I can forgive that."

Penny placed her hand on my arm. "And what about your new suitor?"

I thought for a moment before answering. "Rob is lovely. He's smart, he's handsome, he's fun, kind and caring... but I still don't know what to do, because there's someone else in the mix as well."

"Who is dat, child?" Penny asked.

"David," I replied, gauging her face for a reaction.

She sat there for a moment as I watched her expression change from one of confusion, to slight understanding, and then to mortification.

"David? As in your ex-husband, David?" Penny asked, her eyes wide in disbelief.

"Yes, but it's nothing serious, and it sort of came out of the blue. We just sort of... erm, have been 'getting together' every now and then, if you know what I mean?" I squirmed.

"Oh, Miss. Eleanor!" Penny exclaimed, standing up from her chair. "You cannot be serious! He took everything from you!" She walked away, stopping at the kitchen island, before gasping and turning back to me. "Do you love him?"

"No, no!" I protested. "It's not like that. I think he would like things to be more serious, but I'm just ruing the day that I ever started anything like that up! Even though I do believe he has changed, a part of me can never forget what he's done! But he is always edging for something more, and I wish I would never have gotten involved now. Stephen hates him, and Tasha... boy, if she ever found out. He is the father to my nephew! I can see this all blowing up into one big mess!"

"Oh, Miss. Eleanor," Penny spoke as she came and sat back down again. "I don't even know what to tell you to do."

"I don't know, either. I suppose I'll have to speak to Rob first and see what he says. I keep remembering what you told me about breaking things down, and dealing with one thing at a time, so maybe that's how I'll have to deal with this."

"Who will you choose?" Penny wondered.

'I'm not choosing David. He's too volatile, and he'll be working for me soon. I wish Caroline hadn't even suggested it now, but I've got to let him down gently. I could never go back there. I don't think I trust him at all in a relation-ship sense. As for Stephen... well, he doesn't want me anymore, so I will have to file for divorce. I do really like Rob, and I think he's good for me as well, so maybe giving things a go with him is the best option?" I wondered.

"There you go!" Penny smiled. "Just know, though, that we are all here for you if you need us. You will make the right decision in time... everything works out the way it should do."

"Thanks." I smiled back. "That does mean a lot to me." As we sat with each other for a moment in a comfortable silence, the doorbell rang. "I'll get that." I motioned to Penny, as she went back to the dishes she was doing, and I wan-dered into the hallway to answer the door.

Neatening myself up, I braced myself before answering it. As I opened the door, Brandon was stood there instead.

"Oh, hi, Brandon." I smiled, with my eyes looking to either side of him to see if he was alone.

"Morning, Eleanor. You look disappointed to see me." He chuckled, noting my reaction.

"No, no, it's not that, I was expecting someone else," I replied, trying to look at least a bit happy upon seeing him. "Come on in."

Opening the door wider, I motioned for him to enter. He walked into the house, removing his sunglasses, and I ushered for him to go into the living room. Taking one last look around the driveway, and noting that Rob, thank-fully, wasn't with him, I closed the front door and followed him on behind.

"So what do I owe the pleasure?" I asked, wandering through to where Brandon was now sitting on the sofa.

"Nothing. I thought I would drop by and see how you are." He smiled.

"I'm good, yeah. Well, getting there." I smirked, taking a seat.

"Good, good. I know you were a bit in shock last night, but I must say, it was a complete success. Here..." Brandon sat forward and pulled out a newspa-per from his back pocket.

Taking the newspaper from him, I looked at the front page. Front and cen-tre, the Rose Designs bash had been placed as the event of the year that the most prestigious had attended.

"Wow," I mouthed, as I scanned the article, and looked at the photo of myself and David as we posed on the red carpet. "I didn't think it would capture this much interest."

"If you look at the many famous names that attended, the media were impressed. Good job." He grinned.

"I think a lot of this was mainly down to Caroline, although I did invite a few billionaires that had used our services."

"It's not what you know, it's who you know." Brandon winked.

"Yeah... I'm amazed it all came off so well." I grinned.

As I scanned the newspaper, the doorbell rang again. Engrossed in what the media had reported about the event, I hazily wandered to the front door and opened it. As I looked up, I was met by the sight of David stood at the other side of the threshold.

"Hi, El." He grinned, and even before I asked him whether he wanted to come in, he stepped through.

"Erm, hi." I smiled shakily, wondering what the hell he was doing here.

"You never knew how to greet a guest." He chuckled, turning to me in the hallway.

"What are you doing here?" I wondered, clinging onto the newspaper in my hand.

"I actually came over to see whether you'd seen that," he replied, pointing at the newspaper. "The night went really well."

"Yeah, it did, thank goodness." I smiled in relief.

"Listen, El..." David edged closer to me, and took my free hand in his, "I was looking at that photo of us today. We do look great together..."

Just before he could finish what he was saying, Brandon emerged from the living room and let out a little cough of interruption. David looked up from me, and his eyes narrowed at the sight of Brandon stood in the doorway.

"Oh, er, I didn't realize you had company," David stated through gritted teeth.

"Yeah, I was just going to say that I'll get going and leave you to your day," Brandon spoke as he walked toward me.

Wanting to escape the situation of David asking for more than I was willing to give, I didn't really want Brandon to leave. At some point I had to let David down, but I didn't want it to be today. He was due to start work for me on Monday, and I didn't want relationships to be soured before then.

"No, no, it's fine. Stay. I'll get Penny to bring us through some iced tea." I smiled, skipping along to the kitchen, as David looked at me like I had ten heads, and Brandon even looked a little awkward.

As I entered the kitchen, I leant back on the wall and took a little breath. Penny, who was making lunch, looked over at me.

"Is everything okay, child?" she asked, scanning me over.

"Yeah, it's just David and Brandon are here at the moment, so I need some iced tea," I stated.

"Iced tea?" Penny replied looking amused.

"Yes, a pitcher of it, please, with three glasses. I know that there's nothing going on with me and Brandon, but I don't want him to leave and me be stuck with David. He was about to ask me to get serious with him again. I need to let him down gently," I muttered, trying to make sense of the situation myself.

"Okay, I'll bring it through," Penny replied, looking baffled.

On the way back to the living room, which it looked like they had both gone into, I mentally berated myself for making a mess of things again. I decided that I would offer them both a drink, and then make my excuses, saying I was busy today - that should work. Then I would have been both polite to Brandon, and not had to encounter any more awkward 'I want more' conversations with David.

As I walked in, Brandon was sat on the recliner and David was sat on the sofa, looking toward Brandon in a strange way, and honestly, you could have cut the atmosphere with a knife.

"So..." I began, trying to cut the tension, "Penny is bringing the iced tea through for us now." I smiled as I sat on the sofa - the other end of it to keep my distance from David.

For a moment we all sat there with the silence saturating the room. I don't think anybody knew what to say, but as long as things were kept polite, they could have a drink and be on their way. Perfect plan.

Penny brought the drinks through for us and scanned the room, not really knowing whether to say anything or not. I smiled and thanked her as she left the tray on the coffee table, and then quickly vacated. As I filled our glasses,

I wished I could have followed Penny, and stayed with her until (especially) David sodded off, but I knew I couldn't do that. Pity.

"So are you doing anything today?" I politely asked Brandon, handing him a drink first.

"Er, no," Brandon replied, taking his glass from me with a sense of awkwardness in his tone. "Saturday is generally my only day off. On a Sunday I'm always prepping for the following working day."

Smiling his way, I then handed David his drink, as the silence fell over us once again. David sat forward in his seat, took his glass, and tried to edge a bit closer to me, looking like he was going to say something.

"Yeah, I'm going the gym soon, so I can't be too long today. It's been lovely to see you both," I fake-smiled, cutting David off in his tracks.

"You? Going the gym?" David smirked. "Haven't you got one in the house?"

"Er, yeah. I don't mind a quick go on the treadmill every now and then, and prefer getting out of the house to do so," I lied - I hated the gym and everything about it.

Before anyone could say anything in reply, the doorbell rang again. I knew that there was a strong possibility it was Rob - just when I thought this situation couldn't get any more awkward - so I decided to ignore it. Brandon and David eyed me strangely when I wasn't moving to answer the door, but I politely smiled and sipped my drink, as if to say, "is there a problem?".

No such luck. Before I could even protest to opening it, Penny had scuttled along the hallway and answered the door. I had completely forgotten to tell her that if anyone else was to ring the doorbell, we were to ignore it. I secretly rolled my eyes, as I could hear Penny greeting someone, and I wondered what to do next.

Just before I could contemplate my next steps, Rob came wandering through the living room door, grinning from ear to ear and holding a huge bunch of crystal-encrusted roses. Upon seeing that I was not alone, his face dropped, and I'm fairly sure that mine did, too.

"Hi, Rob." I stood up, trying to act normal. "How lovely to see you."

David looked like he was about to burst on the sofa, and it was probably fair to say that Brandon didn't know what to do with himself, either.

"Hi, Eleanor," Rob hesitantly replied, eyeing the situation before him.

"Are they for me? They're beautiful," I remarked, trying to act nonchalant, as he cautiously handed the bouquet over to me while eyeing David and Brandon.

"Good to see you, Rob," Brandon stated, standing up and looking a little annoyed at seeing him here, but nevertheless shaking his hand.

"Brandon," Rob stated, sternly shaking his hand back.

"So..." I began, "would you like an iced tea, Rob?"

"Er, well... I was wondering..." Rob mumbled.

"I'll get you a glass," I cut in, skipping toward the kitchen again to escape for a moment, or two.

I raced around the kitchen wall and leant back on it again.

"Miss. Eleanor, everything okay?" Penny asked for the millionth time today.

"No, not really, Penny," I replied with urgency and walked over to her. "I've now got Brandon, David, and Rob all in that room, and it's awkward to say the least!" I whispered. "I know it's not your fault, I forgot to say before, but if the doorbell goes, do not answer it," I urged.

"Isn't it a bit late now? They are all here!" Penny gasped.

I rolled my eyes. "I know that, but, I don't know... if anyone else comes, Tasha or the likes, just keep them away."

"Okay, but are you expecting anyone else?" she wondered.

"No, thank goodness." I sighed, although still reeling from the mess that was in the living room.

"I've got a delivery of groceries arriving soon, so don't worry if you hear me at the door again," Penny reassured.

"Brilliant, thanks. Anyway, I need an extra glass." I smiled. "I better get back in there."

Penny chuckled while handing me a glass, and I reluctantly headed back to the living room to face the man-mess that was present. Considering that Saturday's were usually uneventful, this one was definitely going down in the history books. I had a man who I'd flung myself at, a man who I was sleeping with, and another man that I was dating - all sat in the same room like one big bunch of happy campers. And that's not how it was turning out at all.

Entering the living area, the air was thick with tension, with Rob joining the awkward group dynamics. I smiled sweetly at them all, and then proceeded to fill Rob's glass with iced tea and hand it to him. At this point I actually didn't know what to say to anyone, and I thought to myself that if I was one of the men in this situation, I would have made an excuse to leave by now - but they all seemed glutton for punishment.

Grabbing my glass, I sat on an armchair at the side of the where they were all sitting, and looked on. What did anyone do in this scenario? I did internally chuckle to myself about how this would be great viewing for daytime television, yet it would probably be one of the quietest encounters that had ever been filmed. People would probably watch on in awe, to see who snapped first.

Then it dawned on me - this was not what anyone would've described as being a friendly gathering - this was a battle of egos between these males. A set of antlers each with some butting heads, and we'd have been sorted.

"Did Penny tell you I'd called earlier on?" Rob quietly asked, with David and Brandon immediately turning to him.

If looks could've killed, then it'd already be man down by now.

"Yes, she did," I replied, with the sudden silence cutting any hope of further conversation short again.

Rob lightly smiled and went back to sipping his drink.

Oh my word - just leave! Why would anyone make themselves sit through this? If I didn't live here, I would have long left by now. They all needed to learn some tact and piss off to leave me to enjoy a peaceful day, and the memory of something I could probably laugh at, in five or ten years' time.

"Eleanor, I think it's best that I get going," Brandon stated, placing his glass down and rising from the recliner.

Finally - someone with a bit of sense!

"Aw, so soon? Well, thanks for coming." I smiled. Just as Brandon was about to say goodbye, the doorbell rang again. "Oh, that's groceries for Penny. You might want to stay here a minute, while the delivery comes through the door."

"Oh, er, okay," Brandon replied, looking a bit disappointed that he wasn't able to run away faster.

I stayed standing with him - there was no way I was going to offer him to sit back down again. As I listened in, I could hear the footsteps of Penny make their way along the hallway and open the front door. I could hear the faint sound of her talking to someone, but I couldn't make out what was being said.

I just wanted her to get the groceries through the door like lightning, so I could at least release one male from this misery.

All of a sudden the living room door burst open, and we all turned our heads to see who it was. Panting and dishevelled, my breath hitched when I saw who was stood there - Stephen.

"Eleanor!" he panted.

Penny came darting in after him. "Miss. Eleanor, I tried to stop him!" she exclaimed.

My eyes darted from her to Stephen in disbelief.

"Why are you trying to stop me from entering my own home?!" Stephen cried out toward Penny.

That statement snapped me back to attention.

"Don't you speak to Penny that way!" I yelled.

Stephen whirled his head back around to face me. Then he noticed the three males that were present in the room. By this time, I was still stood next to Brandon, while both Rob and David had risen from their seats.

"What the hell is going on?!" Stephen bellowed, scanning the scenario.

I turned to Penny who looked furious, but even like she didn't know what to do.

"You can leave us, Penny. Thank you for trying to do what I asked of you." I smiled in a reassuring way to her, as she promptly left the room.

Next, I turned to face Stephen - a large part of my heart leaping out at the mere sight of him. But this man had also badly hurt me, and with it being so raw, I couldn't forget.

"What's going on in here is absolutely none of your concern!" I raged.

Stephen stepped forward. "I came back here to walk to my *wife*, and I find her in our living room with three other men! One of which I know only too well!" he shouted, glaring at David. "What the hell is he doing here?!"

This day had just gone from awkward to bad in the space of thirty seconds, and while I wanted to shrivel up into a ball and pretend I wasn't here, Stephen's ludicrous entrance demanded that I be strong. Not only was he being a hypocritical bastard, but he was offending three men that I did respect - a little including David.

"What David is doing here is really none of your concern!" I shouted back. "Where the hell have you been, eh? Out for a carton of milk?!" I watched as

Stephen looked like he wanted to shrivel into a ball now. "You have left both me and your children, and you have the audacity to walk through that door and demand answers! I have nothing to say to you!" I fumed.

"But, Eleanor..." Stephen protested, his arms outstretched toward me.

"I think it's best we leave," Brandon stated.

Stephen's face whirled around toward him. "You were that guy who picked her up from the house one night... have you been sleeping with my wife?!" he yelled, edging towards Brandon.

Brandon smirked and stood firmly in place. "I really wouldn't go there with me."

"What is that supposed to mean?" Stephen sneered, squaring up to him.

"Enough, Stephen! No, I have not been sleeping with Brandon!" I yelled, pulling him back by the arm.

"He hasn't, but I have," David stated, glaring at Stephen.

Stephen swiftly turned to David, and then to me, looking more of a pasty shade of green at those words. He seemed to take a moment to process the words, but eventually he faced me.

"Please tell me he is lying, Eleanor," Stephen quietly stated.

Closing my eyes, I hung my head. I was never any good at lying, so no matter what I did, it would give the game away. Before anyone could say anything else, Stephen lunged toward David and hit him hard in the jaw, sending him flying back onto the sofa as he gripped him by his collar.

"I'm gonna kill you, Sommers!" he raged, as a grapple between them both took place.

I stood there in shock, as both Rob and Brandon lunged toward them, dragging Stephen off David, and holding him back. Stephen angrily fought to get nearer to David to finish the job, but with both men holding him back, he was powerless to do so. David rose off the sofa, clutching his jaw with his hand.

"It's been years since I've had one of them." He chuckled, wincing at the pain of being hit.

"You go near my wife again, and I'll fucking kill you!" Stephen yelled.

Breaking free of my trance, I went over to David.

"Are you okay?" I asked, scanning his jaw.

"I'll live. It's probably best I'm not here. Are you going to be okay with him?" David glared at Stephen.

"Yeah, I'll be fine," I replied, shooting a look of disgust toward Stephen. "I'll see you on Monday."

David left the room and I turned toward Stephen, who was still being held back by both Rob and Brandon.

"I don't believe this!" Stephen shouted. "Get off me!" he growled as he struggled, trying to get his arms out of their grip.

"Do you want us to let him go, Eleanor?" Brandon asked, keeping a firm grip on him.

"Yes, but only if he promises to play nice!" I yelled at Stephen.

"Fine," Stephen simmered, as Rob and Brandon slowly let him out of their grasp.

Straightening themselves up, they were the next to approach me.

"I think it's best we go, Eleanor," Rob stated, his crystal blue eyes looking both war weary and confused.

"Yes. I'm so sorry about this, Rob. I understand if I don't hear from you." I sighed.

Rob nodded in my direction and walked away, with Brandon running a hand down my arm in a gesture of goodbye, and giving me a light smile to tell me that he hoped I was okay.

As I heard the front door click behind them, my heart sank a little. I knew that at some point I would probably see Brandon again, as he had proven on more than one occasion what a true friend he really was. As for Rob, I knew that I would probably never see him again. That kind, handsome gentleman, who did deserve much better than this, was now no longer an option for me, thanks to my estranged husband's temper.

My attention soon turned to Stephen who was stood in front of me, calmed down and looking sheepish.

"How bloody dare you!" I yelled.

"Eleanor, I..." he muttered, looking at the floor.

"No! How dare you come back here and make a scene like that! I have never been so embarrassed and ashamed in all my life!" I raged.

Stephen looked up. "Embarrassed?! Ashamed?! My God, Eleanor! I've just found out that my wife has been sleeping with that animal, Sommers! Have you completely lost your mind?!" he angrily shouted.

"Well..." I mumbled, and then it dawned on me. "Hang on a minute... a lecture from the man who walked out on his wife and children!! I haven't heard from you in weeks!! And then last night... oh, by the way, how is Darcy?!" I spat.

"Eleanor..." Stephen repeated, lowering his head again.

"Oh no, don't stop there! You are highly embarrassed by me, are you?! How about explaining to your children where daddy is when you haven't got a fucking clue!" I glared, now beyond angry.

"How are the children?" Stephen quietly asked.

"Fine! No thanks to you!! You just walked out and left them!! I thought I knew you, but I was obviously mistaken! Tell me, Stephen, how's life with the new woman?! Not great if you are stood in the middle of MY living room!!"

Seething with rage, the adrenaline pumped through my veins. I had never lost it with him before, but something inside me had snapped. Raising my arm, with one swift pelt, I slapped him hard across the face. I was angry, I was hurt, and even with a slap that could never mimic his strength, he was going to feel some of my pain.

Stephen lifted his hand to his face as he looked at me shocked - the finger marks edging across his cheekbone.

"I'm so sorry," he whispered.

I didn't know whether to laugh or cry at that statement. I had just hit him, yet he was apologizing to me! But I knew the apology wasn't about that, and no matter what, he deserved a slap for the way I had been treated. I huffed in temper at him and abruptly sat myself on the sofa; the sofa which was looking dishevelled after he had flung David onto it.

"Sorry for what?" I glared. "Leaving your children, or pissing off on me with no contact as to where you were, or what had happened! Or leaving me to go through a miscarriage alone!" I shouted, feeling the rising lump of hurt in my throat.

The adrenaline was wearing off and was being overtaken by upset. I lowered my head as I felt the tears trickle down my cheeks. I didn't care if he saw me cry - he could be witness to the suffering that he had put me through. I may have thought in the past that I was a strong woman, and thought I could cover up getting over him by sleeping with David, and dating Rob, but he had hurt me more deeply than any other man ever had.

"Oh, Eleanor," Stephen softly whispered, as he sat down on the sofa next to me and put his arm around my shoulders.

For a moment I caved, as my face sank into his chest, my hand gripping his t-shirt, and I sobbed my heart out. I don't think I had properly given myself chance to grieve for the loss of my baby, or my husband. I could smell his familiar scent, I could feel his warmth, as he wrapped me in the comfort of his arms - and then I remembered. I remembered his betrayal, with Darcy's face filling my vision, and what he had done.

I pushed him away. "Get off me!" I snapped, pulling back and wiping my tears away with my hands.

"Eleanor, I'm so sorry I wasn't here for you. God knows, I've always tried to be. I hated myself when my mom told me what had happened. I still hate myself now for what I have put you through."

Looking at Stephen, I saw a little trickle of a tear fall down his cheek. The last time I had witnessed that, was after his car crash and he thought there was a chance he could lose his family. As much as I hated him right now, a part of me still loved him, and I didn't even like to witness that tear.

Sniffing back the rest of my tears, I sat up straight to face him.

"Why are you here, then? For weeks there has been nothing, and then you literally waltz through those doors and wreak havoc in a matter of minutes. Even when I have spoken to your mom, she can't understand your behavior. We all thought we knew you better," I sniffled, fighting back the last of my upset.

"I spoke to my mom, and she told me what had happened with the baby. It was the last straw. I tried to keep away from you and the children... I thought it was for your own good. You say you don't know me, and for a while I didn't know myself," he sullenly replied.

"So if I wouldn't have suffered a miscarriage, you would have never come back? That's no reason to come back here and demand to be accepted again!" I snapped.

"It's not like that, and yes, I would have come back. Truth be told, I was highly ashamed of myself, and I just couldn't come near you. I was threatened with the truth, and in the end I realized that I had to be honest with you."

"You're not making any sense."

Stephen sighed and lowered his head. "It's not as cut and dry as you would think, but I may as well tell you, because I have lost you anyway."

"Out with it, Stephen."

He looked back up at me. "I slept with someone else."

I could feel that pang of hurt again, but I knew that had happened anyway.

"I know. That was a given. So I'm meant to just forgive and forget because you told me that?" I impatiently replied.

"No, of course you're not. But it was the circumstances of it all."

"Oh, please!" I exclaimed, standing up. "Spare me the gory details! I don't want to hear how it went, how she was... I'm assuming we are talking about Darcy?!"

Stephen stood up to face me, and held me by the arms. "Yes, it was Darcy. But you don't understand..."

"What is there to understand?" I glared. "You cheated on me with David's sister!"

"Hypocrite, Eleanor. You've been sleeping with her brother!" Stephen replied, looking angered.

"Yes, well... maybe we are both hypocritical, but I didn't do it whilst I thought we were still together! I don't understand why I need to hear all this!" I protested - him still holding me by the arms, as if forcing me to listen.

"Because Darcy is not just David's sister... she is Kelsie, my ex. The one from New York, who I told you about when we first went to Paris. The one who ran off with her professor?" he prompted.

Racking my memory for a moment, yes, I remembered. I remembered him telling me that she was his first love and 'the one he would never forget'. Well, he didn't waste any time in getting reacquainted with her!

"So you have been sleeping with your ex?! Does that make this any better?! I remember you talking about her, and how she broke your heart! She was your first love, right?! Nice to know I've been replaced by a used model!" I seethed. "Anyway, she has been hanging around Tasha like a bad smell, so how come she didn't say anything?!"

Stephen let go of my arms and sat back down. "Tasha was too young to remember when I was with her. She won't have known what she looked like. Plus, with her changing her name, it wouldn't have clicked with Tasha. Anyway, we have both done wrong with exes, haven't we?" He arched an eyebrow my way.

I sat back down next to him. "Don't try and justify your behaviour with that. Anyway, who said anything about it being wrong?" I huffed.

Stephen shuffled closer to me. "You can't seriously mean that. You're not back with him, are you?"

I sighed. "No, I'm not, but it really has nothing to do with you. You had walked out on me when that happened!"

"But you are still my wife, Eleanor!" he snapped.

"Well you should have thought about that when you had your pants around your ankles!" I shouted.

Stephen sighed. "I deserved that. But as I was saying before, the circumstances weren't how you would expect them to be."

"Ugh... pray tell, what hotel did you shack up in, or did you go back to hers?" I spat.

"I can't remember," Stephen stated.

"What do you mean, you can't remember?" I frowned.

"That's exactly it. I don't remember. I went out with a couple of friends for drinks when me and you weren't talking to each other. I felt like crap, and I needed to let off some steam. The night when we first saw Kel... I mean, Darcy, on that yacht, it brought up some pretty bad stuff that I wanted to forget. So anyway, that night I was out with friends, I ran into her. She was all over me, and I wasn't interested... I loved you. But then she insisted on talking about old times, and how it would be good for us to get along for Reece's benefit. I sat and had a drink with her. The rest of the night was hazy, and I vaguely remember some stuff. Although I was really drunk, and honestly, at one point, I thought it was you I was with! But when I woke up in the morning, it was her next to me in the bed. I couldn't believe it! I was disgusted with myself."

I shuddered at the thought - I had been given a little more information than I'd wanted to hear.

"So you just left me and your family and didn't say anything?" I huffed.

"She had pictures of that night, and was threatening me with them. She was going to show you and I did not want you to see that. She probably only did it to get back at me. She's really vindictive, Eleanor. There's a lot you don't know about her."

"Oh well, I know that. Since you've been gone, she's made out she is best buddies with me - the gall of the woman! If I saw her now, I'd be tempted to rip her head off! What an absolute schemer!" I seethed.

Thinking over things for a moment, I remembered about the transfers made from Stephen's bank account.

"Were you giving her money?" I wondered.

"Yes." He lowered his head again. "I'm so sorry to have used the money that way. She was saying that if I didn't pay up, then she would show you those pictures. I didn't want you here, alone, and in receipt of them. I wanted to be honest with you, and tell you exactly how things had happened."

I sighed. "I don't care about the money. But where have you been staying? And it doesn't excuse the fact that you walked out. Why didn't you just tell me, straight off, what was going on?"

"I've honestly been staying with a friend. And I didn't tell you because it's never that simple with her. She has another streak, Eleanor, and I know her... she gets inside your head. She got inside mine. When she was bribing me she was bringing up stuff from the past, and telling me things I didn't want to hear... things she told me she was going to tell you. It got to the point where I wondered whether you and the children were actually safe to be around me."

He paused, as I reached over and lay a hand on his. He was nowhere near forgiven for anything, but from what I could gather, Darcy had somehow done a real number on him, and that made my blood boil. For some reason she was trying to rob Stephen of any happiness, and that I couldn't understand.

"Why wouldn't we be safe around you? Through the years, that's the one thing I have always been certain of, is being safe around you," I reassured.

"I know, and that's what eventually snapped me out of it, and why I knew I had to come back. I doubted myself, but I would do anything to protect you and our children."

"So what are you talking about?" I asked, eyeing him for a response.

"You really want to know?" he wondered.

"Yes."

The world stood still, as Stephen braced himself to tell me something that seemed to be difficult to spit out. I knew it was burdensome for him, as he wrapped his thumb around my fingers that were placed on his hand.

As he opened his mouth and uttered the words, my blood ran cold.

"Eleanor, I killed someone."

To be continued...

Thank you for reading 'Trials: Live and Learn, Book Four'!
If you enjoyed this book, please leave a review - thanks!
Next in the series:
'Tribulations: Live and Learn, Book Five'
You can find the author at:
www.facebook.com/AmandaVintBooks/[1]
Other titles by this author include:
Hearts Across the Sea
Forbidden
Christmas in Havenstock
Leaving it Late
Lucky Me! series
To Have or To Hold series
Christmas at Clevenden Cottage

Printed in Great Britain
by Amazon

29633305R00096